HORSES,
DIVORCES
& hissy fits

HORSES,
DIVORCES
& hissy fits

TINA CRYER

Forelock Books

Published by Forelock Books Ltd.

24 Lower Street, Pulborough,
West Sussex. RH20 2BL

www.forelock-books.co.uk

First published in 2016

Printed by Bell & Bain Ltd., Glasgow, UK
Typeset by lksdesigns.co.uk
Edited by Rose Fox

A CIP catalogue record for this book is available from the British Library

ISBN 978-0-9954652-1-3

For Toby, who left hoofprints on my feet and on my heart.

Chapter 1

Imagine: a remote country retreat set down a long leafy lane; a charming olde worlde cottage with roses round the door, lupins and hollyhocks in the garden.

NOT!

Truth is, we are living in a building site. The air is thick with dust of centuries-old plaster, dirt, rotting wood, and a zillion corpses of every living creature from flies to wood-worms. This noxious fug is destroying our lungs, clogging our pores, and probably laying down the foundations of a painfully slow death in later life.

My mother is seriously deranged; she waltzes round shouting "Isn't it FanTASTic!" and "It's a dream come TRUE!"

Oh! Purleez!

Normal people have floors. We have holes; we have piles of wood, heaps of rubbish, bags of cement and plaster, layers of polythene and an assortment of lethal, sharp and dangerous tools. Every step we take is part of an obstacle course of life-threatening proportions. If we don't die of suffocation in some deep stagnant pit we've fallen into, we'll die of twitching, hair-raising electrocution; because we don't have neat little spotlights, we have lightbulbs dangling at head height from bare wires. Our electrical sockets aren't glued to the wall like in any ordinary house – oh no! too simple – we have ONE socket dangling from a swinging wire, and that has to serve all our needs from kettle to hair dryer to telly, and even the army of builders' power tools.

My mother – my insane only-parent* - is in Heaven because "It's all HAPPENING!"

Yeah! Right! Oh yippy-do!

(* will explain this later. I used to have two parents but I divorced my father).

'You can always go into the caravan' she shrugs aside my objections. I up the odds, throw worse tantrums, sulk for longer, shout and even risk the odd bit of swearing but NO! she is obliviously happy, deliriously joyful. Nothing shall spoil her excitement.

'CARAVAN: company travelling together for safety.' Hmmm!

Our caravan was bought in haste from a shonky dealer who saw the bliss of new-house passion in my mother's eyes and charged accordingly. It was bought to give us refuge from the noxious chemicals involved in turning our cottage from a derelict eyesore into a candidate for Ideal Homes magazine. We curled up in it when the woodworm was treated and again when a damp-proofing 'thing' was done.

As a place of safety if COULD be usable by the most vertically-challenged of pygmies. Nothing is normal human-being sized. The beds are just about big enough for your average four year old. It came, at no extra cost, complete with a range of projections designed to decapitate anybody over a metre tall.

And it stinks. Maybe cats once lived (and peed) in it; or there could be something that's sort-of dead hidden in it. I don't know, for despite mother's use of elbow grease with a combination of Jeyes Fluid and Cillit Bang's full range, it's no better.

Revered parent may have filled the cupboards with an

assortment of goodies to distract attention from its peculiar smell and lack of cat-swinging space... Am I fooled?

Nah! As I munch my way through chocolate bars and crisps, I can still smell the smell and know that whether I stand still or move, it's Sod's Law that I shall fracture my skull, or at least dislocate an elbow. Does the parent care? Nope! She's frolicking round the garden revelling in dewy grass and singing some soppy song about gathering lilacs.

Yeah! Right!

Re-reading this, I realise I actually sound quite amused despite the grumbling. I sound like 'oh-ho, ah-ha... it's all good fun really'. This is quite surprising in view of the fact that not one single aspect of this situation is amusing. There is not a glimmer of laughter in my whole being.

I AM ANGRY!!!!

Seriously. I may well be developing Tourette's Syndrome: in my head the internal dialogue is just a mush of swearing. Every thought is interspersed with language so foul, even I didn't know I could be so poisonous.

An alien being has transplanted itself into my head. It reeks, exudes evil, has no humour and exists only to hurt others verbally or physically. All things bad and crude and wicked combine to create its nasty, dark soul.

I want to know where 'I' went to leave room for this Awful Thing.

Text to Kim:

> U wd laff 2 c
> hovel we live
> in. Buck Palas
> it aint.
> Workmen r all
> at least 90.

But my thumb must have been working on instinct. I couldn't see the keypad for the tears in my eyes.

Hacking a hedge to bits is my Penance. I'd love to prune it neatly with one of those electric hedge-trimmers, but in the absence of anything that sophisticated, I'm lopping thorny branches off, alternating with secateurs and a small (supposedly sharp but in reality very blunt and rusty) curved jobbie with a wooden handle.

I can list a hundred things I'd rather be doing, and they range from lying on a sun-drenched beach to poking barbed wire under my nails. Trouble is, after our huge row this morning, Mum switched on the windscreen wipers as she drove the car out of the drive. I knew she was crying because it wasn't raining.

Even with this Malevolent Thing inhabiting my body, there remain some crumbs of conscience. So this pruning lark is by way of apology for some… I must admit it… unforgivably cruel things I said.

Parents! Pah! They take some training, don't they?

Why decimate a perfectly innocent hedge? I hear you ask.

It's like this…

My beloved parent, finding herself single after fourteen years paired with a control-freak, is rediscovering her 'Self'. Or something!

She's too young to have been a Hippie or a Flower Child in the 60's, but that's the impression she creates. Dancing barefoot in the dew, tree hugging and conversing with the moon draw her, she claims, into her feminine side.

Yeah! Right!

So while she embraces her Inner Child and aspires to being an Earth-Goddess, I explore my Inner Monster and aspire, in my darker moments, to being an Orphan.

So… the hedge…!

In her new persona, my parent is planning on living The Good Life. Maybe not going as far as filling the house with Vietnamese Pot-bellied pigs, but at least being able to shake compost off the carrots before grating them.

In our new garden, what was once a vegetable plot has succumbed to years of weeds and their offspring, and the hedge alongside it has assumed Sleeping Beauty proportions. The hedge needs some serious attention before the vegetable plot can be dug and manured and sown with the varieties of happy little plants that will make for a happy little mum.

So there you have it. My Inner Monster (hereafter to be known as I.M.) has snoozed for long enough to allow my guilt to do some lopping by way of apology.

I really didn't mean to accuse her of driving away my father.

In reality, the only thing that did that was whatever he keeps in his trousers.

Moi? Bitter?

Oh-ho… I feel an attack of Tourettes coming on…

My dream of a beautifully manicured symmetrical bank of green hedge is fast turning into a nightmare. Like Paddington Bear cutting down the height of a table, leg by leg, I find myself drawn back to bits I've already lopped in order to level and smooth. The tools I'm using don't exactly encourage finesse and artistry. One hacks, one bleeds, one creates another ragged hole in the hedge, one moves on, tweezing thorns out of blood-spattered hands and arms…

"You need some shears" remarks Eric the Electrician who has come outside for a smoke.

"I know that. I don't have any" I answer crossly.

"Have you looked in the shed?" he blows a cloud of smoke across the garden.

Truth is. No. I haven't looked round the sheds, the garden or even the house because I don't want to BE HERE. AND

I don't want Mum to think I have the LEAST INTEREST in the place. If I don't acknowledge its existence it may go away, vanish, vamoosh…

"Couldn't find any" I lie.

"Sure I saw some" he muses, trudging across what was once lawn in his big brown boots. I wait, praying he won't find any even though I could use them…

"Aye… thought so…"he's dripping ash from his cigarette down the blue T shirt stretched over his bulging beer belly, and waving a pair of rather rusty shears aloft.

"Don't know how I missed them" I lie, smiling sweetly.

Holding them at eye level, he snaps them open and closed experimentally. "Need oiling" he forces them open, and holding them out like a cross, disappears into the house in search of lubricant. I croon softly to my shredded and bleeding arms.

Edward Scissorhands reappears, and with a flourish, his flashing hands whip along the hedge so fast I have to leap for safety. I spit out twigs and leaves as he zips past in a cloud of flying foliage.

"Sharp, them" he grins at me as, in no time, he reaches the far end, framed by a bank of smooth green hedge pinched straight from my dream. Even the lacework I'd created with the curved thing and secateurs has been levelled into the whole.

"Good job" I force a smile, peeved that he's ruined my Atonement, but secretly relieved that the hedge is done and if I'm cool, I can con my mother into believing it is all my own work.

Flicking shredded greenery off his shoulders, he hands over the shears. "Bit over there still to do" he nods his head in the direction of the gateway.

"Yup. Right. Thanks" I mutter as graciously as possible,

noticing with rage that he hasn't a single scratch or puncture wound.

Could be good Spin. One glance at my tattered arms will convince the parent it was all my own work. I make a mental note to wear a sleeveless T-shirt to display the evidence.

The maturity with which I handled the situation is probably what impressed Electric Eric and prompted his Scissorhands impersonation. Am I bovvered? At least I got the hedge snipped!

Outside.

Surrounded by trees and grasses and all the unnatural sounds of nature it is unbelievably noisy.

Eric has effortlessly pruned about thirty metres of hedge, leaving me a short stretch of about five metres to finish. It will probably take me the remainder of this year. Or longer.

Snip, snap, snip.

I glance towards the house, feeling a shudder of unseen eyes observing me.

Clink, clunk. Chink.

I could swear I hear heavy breathing.

A radio is belting out Coldplay in the house. That will be Pete the Heat (as my mother calls him) installing the central heating. A shouted conversation is going on between two rough voices – Electric Eric and Rick the Brick. (My mother was so overwhelmed by all the testosterone when a troop of tradesmen requisitioned the house, the only way she could deal with them was to reduce them to the status of cartoon characters. The only one she couldn't demote was Desmond the Joiner).

Between them they exhibit the looks and charm of a herd of very sick hippos. So much for the 'Builders' Bums' that Kim is still fantasising about. As if!

Right on cue, my mobile vibrates in my jeans pocket:

7

Horrid @ Gym without u.
Cum back. Y U not Emailing? Kim

Press Reply. Write:

No elec. No computr.
I miss Gym & am
turning into a fat slob.

As I press 'Send', I hear a distinct snort through the hedge. Definitely.

My eyes roll. I grow wary. Could be a mugger, an axe-murderer, a madman intent on plunder and pillage or…

Approaching the place tentatively, I peer through leaves and twigs, nearly gouging my eyes out in the process and adding new rips to the collection on my arms.

As I stare through the foliage, a pair of eyes peers back at me.

Aaargh!

How far to the house? I glance over my shoulder.

How fast am I? Faster than an ageing pervert? a burglar with sack printed 'swag'?

I shuffle a metre to my right.

The eyes move, following me.

Heavy breathing.

"Don't be stupid" I tell myself. "This is the country. It'll be a cow" but a sneaky thought asks 'Shouldn't it be mooing, then?'

AND

what is it doing in our field?

Carefully, step by step, I move sideways to the gate.

Through the hedge I can hear feet, and grass swishing. I wish the birds would stop their damned racket so I could hear better.

Reaching the gate, I pause and peep round the hedge.

A face appears round the yet untrimmed section beside the gate; a white face with dark brown markings round the eyes. A very long face. No horns (do cows still have horns? I wonder) a long black silky topknot later to be known as a forelock, but at this stage this creature was a glorified cow minus horns and udder.

Yup, dear Reader. You were always one step ahead of me, weren't you? You got it in one, but I'm a proud Townie, born and bred. We who live in towns really genuinely believe that milk comes from supermarkets…

If you are one of those 101% Pony Mad teenagers, you're probably bouncing up and down with excitement.

Not me. I'm afraid the horse-mad phase passed me by while I was at Gymnastics just as learning the piano, dreams of being a pop star, fashion model, supermodel or even being a celebrity just for the fame, ALL passed me by while I was at Gymnastics.

NOT difficult considering I trained five days a week, with competitions on Saturdays and sometimes Sundays. If I had any spare time between Gym and School, I did the odd ballet class to improve my floor routines, or went to weight training to build upper body strength.

Big brown eyes and a soft snuffley muzzle did nothing for me.

All I could think was "What's a horse doing in our field?"

We communicate with the security of a hefty metal five-bar gate between us, this horse and I. My arm stretches out and tentatively slides towards the dark brown neck, but the horse needs to sniff me and reaches his nose forward, breathing through soft nostrils. His muzzle is really hairy – long hairs like a cat's whiskers. Even from a distance they tickle my skin.

Crazy as it may sound, I've never spoken to a horse before; not in my whole life. Apart from the language of touch, I've no idea how to begin. Fortunately, pony seems to have more idea than I, and gentle, warm, slightly moist breath touches the back of my hand.

Oh!

Wow!

Nervously, my fingers stretch towards the hairy neck and, expecting to meet a terrible fate, make contact. The hair is short and coarse; nothing like a cat or a dog or human hair. I push into the hair and feel firm warm skin.

Huge dark eyes regard me without fear or malice. As I begin to stroke, the animal leans into my touch. I have no idea what I'm doing, but it seems to be okay.

A massive front hoof shuffles forward, allowing me to reach all the way down the neck to the bones of the shoulder. The pale muzzle pushes against the gate, seeking my face.

I am silenced with awe.

Nothing like this has ever happened to me before.

I think I must be in love!

Chapter 2

Hearing the sound of wheels on gravel, I dashed round the side of the house to drag my mother to see The Horse before she could get sucked into the Male Hormone Brigade.

"What? what? what?" she was gasping as I grabbed her arm and tugged her over trampled flowerbeds and the cement-covered lawn.

Later I realised she was suffering shock on seeing me a) vertical instead of horizontal b) not glued to wires and headsets, nodding my head moronically to an unheard beat, and c) I cringe to admit – smiling!

"Oh Sara! It's fantastic" she had stopped in amazement on seeing The Hedge. I'd forgotten all about it "Oh not THAT" I shouted grumpily in exasperation.

No, she had to go on "you must have worked so hard"

"Yeah… well… but come ON"

But my mother the Airhead was back, a soppy expression transforming her features. "Isn't it wonderful? Even a trimmed hedge can make such a difference, don't you think? Can you imagine how amazing it will look when the garden is all landscaped… we are so LUCKY"

"Oh for crying out loud!" I snapped, mood broken and excitement seeping away.

"What?" the guarded look she habitually wears around me these days, slid down her face like a dark veil.

"It doesn't bloody matter" I shouted, stamping my foot. (Ooops, I guess I forgot my two second breakthrough into Maturity earlier in the day! Okay, maybe I'll Grow Up tomorrow instead…)

"Sara…" pleading, "how can I KNOW how to behave around you if you don't tell me what the RULES are?"

Huffing out a Drama Queen sigh and rolling my eyes, I capitulated.

"Come on, then" I pushed her towards the gate. Leaning over it, she swivelled her head left and right, surveying our vast estate, actually a paddock roughly the size of a football pitch.

On hearing us, the horse's head shot up, ears pricked and a rumbling noise fluttered from its nose. Never taking its eyes off us, it shuffled towards the gate.

"It's a horse!" my mother marvelled.

Dripping sarcasm because I hadn't forgiven her for shattering my good mood, I mocked "Oh, well done!"

"What's it doing in our field?" she asked, pushing her arm through the bars, hand flat to tempt the horse forward.

"I thought you might know" I said. Mothers are supposed to know EVERYTHING. "We don't want a stupid horse dumped on us, do we?"

"Not stupid…" she breathed as the horse did that huffing, tickling thing to her outstretched hand. "This one, though… is in very poor condition… "

Sick with jealousy, I snatched my own hand back through the gate, so I should never know whether the pony had chosen her hand over mine.

"I reckon it's been dumped here because it's disabled" I muttered darkly.

"Disabled?" Mum glanced at me "What d'you mean?"

"It's a cripple… look at its hideous deformed feet"

"Oh… oh, my goodness… but not crippled… just dreadfully in need of a good farrier"

"A what?"

"Farrier… blacksmith… a pedicure… "

"What do you know about it?" astonished and rather miffed that she knew stuff about horses.

Scratching the hairy neck with her fingernails, she turned to me, laughing. "I used to ride when I was a kid"

"Did you? I never knew that"

"You probably never knew that I also played a clarinet for, oh, at least three months, or that I was thrown out of Brownies because I refused to chant all that stuff about 'God and Queen and doing my duty'. There's a whole lot of stuff you don't know, Sahara, because you don't WANT to know; you don't ask; you choose not to converse… " turning away, she started walking across the dusty untidy lawn "… because you want to fester in your own anger…"

Cor!

That's me told, then.

Text to Kim:

> Aren't parents the pits?
> I wanna cum back 2 town.
> Can I live with u?

One angry parent was swearing at her phone because her battery was flat. I do have some sympathy: our one electrical socket is commandeered all day by Big Men with Power Tools. If we want electricity for something as trivial as recharging phones, we have to get up in the middle of the night. As my phone is my only lifeline to relationships which seem to be fading it is more important than hers, she has a car and can drive to civilisation, is my argument, and I get first charge.

I'm not entirely heartless: I know she's mad at me and only taking out her aggression on the phone. I pass my mobile to her. "Thanks… but on second thoughts…"she says, fixing a very beady eye on me "we'll go into town"

As I start to protest, she says "Not open to negotiation, Sahara. You need school uniform – you start school next Monday – whether you like it or not." Poker-faced my mother, when determined. "We'll get the uniform then sort out the matter of the pony with elongated feet"

I open my mouth to speak, wishing I could wave a wand and spirit her back into Airhead mode but "No arguments! Get ready!"

Tough I may be, but not THAT tough.

Meekly, I get ready.

***

Not a word was spoken in the car on the way into town.

I fiddled with the radio, knowing it annoyed her, flicking through foreign languages and trillions of different musical styles, while she tutted and adjusted the volume.

Steely eyes cautioned me: Mother was in Manager Mode and would take no prisoners; I'll shoot at sight, her extravagant sighs warned me. Had I really mocked her skittish, flouncing, Child of Nature moods? In future I would nurture and encourage them!

In the outfitters shop, she produced the crested list of items I would need in order to integrate at my new school. For three weeks I had assaulted, hidden, discarded and defaced that list but I had under-estimated my mother's knowledge of my perverted character. When the list arrived, she had taken it into her office and made dozens of photocopies. Every time I vandalised one, like a magician whipping bright flowers out of a top hat, she would produce yet another new one – clean, pure and unspoiled. Each time, the look she gave me should have been preserved in the Family Album.

My Policy had been formulated; a Manifesto published. Whatever I was offered would be rejected.

So, I hated the silly blue and red gingham dresses.

I detested the tailored navy shorts.

I loathed the scratchy, navy blazer with an embroidered school motto on the pocket.

The navy skirt was too short... or too long. The white shirts were boring.

I wouldn't be seen dead in a cardigan like that...

Yuk to white knee socks.

Loudly I criticised the shop assistant – I mean 'Yvonne, Sales Adviser', the décor, the smug rails of identical kit, every aspect of the school uniform and literally (ouch! It embarrasses even me!) threw the detested tie on the floor. Though I did stop short at jumping on it!

The parent suffered nobly, exchanging glances with the poor woman who was only trying to set me up with anonymity in my new school.

Mother only calls me Sahara when annoyed; the dialogue was heavily punctuated with Saharas. Yeah, well, stupid name anyway. My friends always shorten it to Sara (on pain of Chinese Burns, otherwise).

Patiently she picked up discarded dresses, skirts, shirts, cardigan, blazer, gym kit, and even the tie.

"This is the deal... " said my mother in a steely cold voice. "I buy these items and you WILL wear them... OR you have exactly one minute to change the selection or find sizes you are happy with. From... NOW..." Pointedly she studied her watch as I scurried round, swapping the hideous gingham dresses for the alternative navy skirt and white shirts. Neatly, I piled all my goods on the counter and gravely told 'Yvonne, Sales Adviser' "We'll take these, please"

Defiantly I glanced at my snotty parent; she was trying so hard not to laugh that her eyes were streaming with tears.

How DOES she do that?

It feels as though she wins EVERY time!

"Plan of action over a cup of tea" Mum ordered as we stashed the horribly expensive pile of bulging carrier bags in the boot of the car.

"With a meringue?" I made it sound like a threat.

"If we MUST". We're both crazy about meringues but, due to financial hardship, only have them on rare special occasions.

Nothing must interrupt the decadent ritual of meringue-scoffing, so we didn't talk until we had both cleaned every smidgin of crumbled meringue off our plates.

"I thought you might want to check out the shopping mall…" Mum observed casually, stirring her tea.

Mentally I counted to ten. How she reads the situation all wrong so consistently amazes me. One (very tiny) mature cell in my brain reminded me that she was trying hard. "Mum…" how to explain? "The malls at home weren't important. They were somewhere to hang out…" She was avoiding my eyes but listening intently. "… it was meeting my mates there that mattered…"

"I thought you shopped." Poor old thing: obviously dementia is setting in.

"Bits of things, yeah…" I said patiently "… and we tried on clothes and picked up any freebies… but it was meeting my friends… dossing about… It was about the only NOR-MAL thing I ever did…" I stopped when I felt something solid lodge in my throat.

"What d'you mean?" asked my mother, seriously per-plexed. Send for the White Coats! She's lost the plot!

"Because I trained so hard. I was at Gym every day. Every spare minute outside Gym I was running… or doing weights… or dance. Have you forgotten!? I got up at six o'clock every morning to do my homework and go for a run." My voice was rising "It was all so HARD!" My throat was clogged with dead leaves.

"It was YOUR choice!"

"I know. I WANTED to do it" my voice sounded exasperated.

"How many times did I beg you to cut back and do less training?" Mum was defensive; as though I was blaming her.

"When I was 'In' it, I guess it was like being on a treadmill. I got on with it; I never questioned whether I wanted to do it…" I met her eyes "I don't blame YOU… except sometimes it was fun to defy you when you nagged about cutting down" colour rushed into my cheeks; I HATE blushing all the time.

"So all that stuff about diet and drinking gallons of water every day… and training every day, and pumping iron, and ballet and skipping… hours and hours every week…" She leaned back in her chair, hand on her forehead; her voice rose in pitch so she was almost shrieking "… are you telling me… are you really saying that was all to get at ME?" incredulously.

I glanced round the café, embarrassed to be with a parent who screeches in public, and hissed "No-o-o!" and after a moment "I also wanted to be really, really good at something"

"But you were torturing yourself if you didn't ENJOY it" Mum held out her hands as though weighing answers between them.

"Enjoy?" I mused on that, then said "I was HUNGRY for it. And… Alison was so hard on us… she was hungry as a trainer. She made me believe that if I was more committed, if I worked harder and longer… that I really could be good enough for the Commonwealth Games" I stopped, blocked by the painful memory of how I had strived for that.

Mum's eyes were full of pain. I could tell she wanted to give me a hug. "And I so… so…" pausing because tears were threatening "wanted Dad to be proud of me… I wanted him to *really* notice me… I thought it would make him LOVE me…"

One of those really soppy mother and daughter moments overwhelmed us and we sat across the cold tea cups and sticky plates with tears rolling down our faces.

"He DID love you, Sara" Mum said at last.

"Not enough to stay with me" I shouted angrily, scraping back my chair and barging clumsily out of the café.

Leaning against the wall of an *Antique Shoppe* down the street, I waited for her, swallowing hard and scrubbing at my face with a tissue.

"Right" said my mother breezily, coming up beside me. Taking my arm as though nothing had happened, she pulled a silly face and said "Let's go and see a man about a horse"

***

Mister Barry Fenton, Property Agent and Valuer, fancied my mother. Fortunately for me, heartily sickened by the very concept of parents and therefore not seeking a replacement father, she referred to him in private as a weasel.

A very charming weasel if you like 'em doused in sickly aftershave, and so tailored and over-ironed that you might feel inclined to rumple him or coat him in something gunky and smelly. And… if you like Charm of the Most Insincere Variety.

"A pony?" puzzled, he bounced around Mum, ushering her with elaborate hand gestures to a chair opposite his large over-tidy desk. "A pony? I know nothing about a pony" I was waiting for him to call her Dear Lady.

Mr Fenton was in the process of growing himself a silky

little gingery moustache to match his short, over-barbered, gingery hair. I felt like saying DON'T, but as I was already verging on silent hysteria, restrained myself. I didn't dare meet Mum's eye; it would be enough to make me erupt into childish giggles. Childish? Moi? I don't think so!

"As you know…" he was saying "The family who lived there left under…" He glanced at me, chose carefully and whispered to Mum "… a cloud"

"They did a runner" she interrupted.

"There were… er… financial problems" he corrected her tactfully.

"Actually… they did a moonlight flit" she declared boldly.

Glancing at me uneasily, as though this topic was not suitable for young ears, he cleared his throat and murmured "There were problems of a… ah… marital nature as well as… um… financial matters"

Oh purleez! "The pony?" I interrupted.

"Ah!"

"Never mind 'ah'" I said rudely, I swear that made his dinky little moustache quiver, "why has some poor malnourished nag been dumped in our field?"

"Excuse me while I get the file on your property" he said, smiling at my mother and holding her stoney glance longer than necessary. I resisted the impulse to ram two fingers down my throat and retch.

"Behave!" my mother mouthed at me as the immaculately pressed suit bent itself over a filing cabinet. Shuffling papers, he sat down opposite us again.

"No mention here of any rental agreements… no references to a horse… vacant possession on completion…" he muttered to himself as papers flickered like butterflies beneath his perfectly manicured fingers.

"So what… " anybody else would have quailed at the

expression in my parent's eyes "is a pony doing in our field?" Pausing, she forced his eyes to her face "… and, more importantly, what are you going to do about it?"

Afterwards, we stood outside the huge window full of pictures and descriptions of properties for sale and giggled like a couple of kids.

"If you marry him, I shall divorce you" I told her.

"If I marry him, you can divorce me and shoot me" replied my hysterical parent, wiping tears from her eyes.

"Not much help was it?"

"No" commented my suddenly sober parent "we still have a horse in our field"

"Heck, yeah" I tutted, but my heart gave a little lurch of joy.

Ambling across the field towards me, the pony nickered softly deep in his throat. He was choosing to be with me and, almost in reverence, I snapped off my iPod and pulled the headphones out of my ears. Wind rushed through trees, leaves stirred and birds shouted noisily in wrap-around sound.

Like meeting a new friend, I felt nervous, afraid of getting it wrong. The pony stopped in front of me and reached out a soft velvety muzzle to sniff my hand. Had I been one of those pony-mad girls I'd have known what to do – what language to use, how to interpret the signs. The only horse I'd known previously was a padded wooden one which didn't communicate.

Tentatively, I stretched out my hand and he didn't back off, but allowed me to touch him. I tried to run my fingers through the scruffy mane but they snagged on knots and tangles. Instead, I gently pushed my hand under the coarse ragged mane onto the warm neck beneath. Growing very quiet, the pony stood still, waiting. I wasn't sure whether the infinitesimal movements of blood and muscle and breath in the contact of skin on skin were his or mine.

How strange, how miraculous that I'd never experienced contact like that before – not with any person or any animal. A sense of wonder filled my head with light.

When I slid my hand to a new position on his neck, he snorted softly down his nostrils, then bent his head to rest his forehead against my upper arm.

Beneath the hair, his skin was warm, though his coat felt coarse and unkempt. For a moment I laid my head against his neck, breathing in the unfamiliar scent of horse. As I brushed my fingers along his shoulder, I revelled in the variations of texture beneath my hand. From the softness of his neck, I traced the bones of his shoulder, located the spine and swept my hand along the ridge of his back.

With a huge sigh, his whole frame appeared to soften; the angular lines of his bones feeling blurred and relaxed.

Between the big muscles of his chest, I could feel his sternum. Running my hand between his front legs, I tuned in, waiting for a heartbeat. And felt it – baddum baddum baddum – amazing to acknowledge this animal's heart pumping blood round his body. When I placed my hand under his belly, I could feel and hear the gurgles and rumbles of his digestion. So personal! I felt truly honoured and rested my face against his chocolate-brown side, hypnotised by the tides of his body effortlessly performing their functions. When I tuned in to his breathing, it felt like my own. Our patterns were so similar, we breathed in harmony. Drifting a little, I was drowsy with the intimacy of such sharing.

My chest filled with a pain so exquisite that my eyes were damp with tears. I hadn't realised it was possible to feel another being in this way. Had I ever, I wondered, been moved or touched by another living being. Had I, in fact, ever really felt anything?

Running my fingers over his rump, I felt his tail, which had been clamped down tight, relax and flick comfortably.

All I'd ever known about horses was that one end could bite and the other end was likely to kick and they were, collectively, responsible for fractures of every conceivable bone. With only a slight hesitation, using firm pressure, I circled my fingers down his back leg. As I reached the mass of hair down the back of his leg, he shifted his weight and appeared willing, in a languid way, to lift his foot. For me, a hoof off the ground was too scary; I moved on, painting every inch of him with my two hands.

Drowsily, he breathed on my hands as I returned to his head and began massaging the other side of his neck. As I stroked and kneaded, I knew this shaggy, dreamy horse had given himself to me – if only in this one moment in our lives.

Hands wallowing in every inch of his rough brown coat, I marvelled at the tenderness I was feeling. There was no selfishness in me; my arms were heavy but my hands knew where they should travel to soothe and comfort him.

Welded together in the moment, all else faded. Maybe birds sang and wind shimmied poplar leaves and traffic hummed distantly, but I heard none of it.

Even the expression on his face had changed. Dreamy eyes wore a faraway look; his muzzle was soft and pliable, bottom lip drooping a little. At times his head dropped so low and so heavy that his breath disturbed the dry powdery soil.

I stroked; he dozed. Light directed my hands and I lulled him, soothed him.

What he was giving me was life changing.

No longer was there one giving and one receiving, there was just a Gift given and received in indescribable loveliness.

Chapter 3

Day begins early on our building site. Our facilities are so basic, we have to make use of whatever we need before the workmen arrive or, as my mad mother puts it,' Before the Germans', which I understand is a racist reference to towels on sun-loungers in exotic locations like Benidorm and Lanzarote. All beyond my experience, I have to say.

Exciting – a bath has been installed and, two days ago we were given the exquisite gift of hot water to fill it with. Alas, no bathroom door. If we wish to be clean, we jump in and out of the bath, hoping any muck will rub off on the towel. In some dreamy perfect future, I'm assured, we shall have a door and also a shower, but many more stages of renovation need to be completed before then.

One eye on the clock, my parent and I chivvy each other in and out of the bath and then rush to make toast and boil the kettle for coffee before the first rusty white van rattles its way down the lane. Once our army of hunks (NOT!) arrive, they 'need' the kettle and, as I've already explained, we are in the reduced circumstances of having to share one electrical socket with just about everybody in the world.

"Ha-ha" gloats my parent "beaten 'em this morning!" as we struggle to make ourselves comfortable in the midget caravan over our cereals, toast with jam, and coffee. Basic as this may sound, it's the nearest thing to a meal we ever have these days. We do have a microwave but it can only be used once all the workmen have trundled their weary bones into their rusty vans and rumbled away home. Even then, hot drinks, re-charging phones and running the washing machine and hair dryer take priority over food. Salad it is then; day after day. You'd be amazed how inventive one becomes when necessary. Did you know, for instance, that cornflakes make a lovely crunchy topping for salads? Cold beans are this season's must-have, and dandelion leaves are full of iron and vitamins? Yeah, well, now you know!

Today is a very auspicious day because the plasterer is due to start. The one thing we have learned about tradesmen is that their idea of 'today' is not necessarily the same as ours; next week can mean anything from tomorrow to three years' time. We do not hold our collective breath; there is no guarantee that Jim will actually remember that today he is coming to make my mother's dreams come true. He is the last link in the chain. I even permit myself some little thrills at the realisation that he is going to start his smoothing work on the walls in what will be my bedroom. For now it is a bare, carpet-less, dusty mess where I unroll a mattress each night so that I don't have to share the midget caravan with my mother.

"I've just remembered" Mum said "I think he's called Teddy"

"Who? the plasterer? I thought he was called Jim?"

"No... not the plasterer. He's Jim. The pony"

"What pony?" Poor thing; she's losing the plot.

"The pony in our field. Duh!"

"How d'you know that? Are you psychic?" Ohmygod! I'm having a conversation with my mother!

"Yeah, right!" she started tidying the pots together ready for washing up. "You know when your Aunty Jen came down to help me move in... well... the garage was full of junk. We needed the garage to store all our stuff in, so that first day all we did was shift all the rubbish out of the garage and into the various sheds"

I was a little embarrassed at this point because I'd absolutely refused to help with any stage of the move and had even gone to stay with my friend Zoe while it all happened. I had even, I blush to recall, refused to pack my own stuff and had left my mother to box all the contents of my room, even my clothes... even... even my most prized CDs and well... everything!

"We'll have to hire a skip and have an almighty clear out when the workmen have finished..."

"... the pony's name...?"

"Oh yes... well... we chucked all their stuff into the shed and when that was full, we started cramming it into the stable..."

"What stable?"

"Hello? Earth to Planet Zog..." My mother waved her hand in front of my face. "The stable... there..." Pushing me to the window she pointed across the dirty garden to a building beyond the lawn.

"Oh" I said. I think I mentioned I have tried to pretend this place doesn't exist; if I don't acknowledge it, it might go away. So I've never walked round the perimeter; never waited for my fond parent to embrace the view with the memorable words 'One day, all that you can see will be yours!' I haven't investigated or marvelled, haven't walked into the lane or explored the area. I could, in fact, be living on Planet Zog. My trip in the car to buy school uniform and talk to the weasly estate agent was the first time I've moved out of the house and garden.

"Teddy?"

"Oh yes… well… on the floor in the stable…"

"How d'you know it's a stable?" I interrupted. "It looks just like a shed" I was a bit miffed that I'd never noticed it; I hate her knowing things like that.

"Duh! A door in two halves, bottom half high enough for a horse to look over… concrete yard… ring to tie a horse to… bales of hay… a pile of buckets… maybe, just maybe, I recognise a stable when I see one" my sarcastic parent swept crumbs off the table into the rubbish bin. "Well as I was saying… in the STABLE - filled with rubbish like every other outbuilding… we found a wooden name plate that said TEDDY. Jen laughed about it and made some rubbish joke about why a teddy bear would need to know its own name…"

"What sort of a wooden name plate?" I asked suspiciously.

Huge sigh. "You can be so tiresome, Sara. The sort of wooden nameplate one might fasten on a stable door so a horse will know what it's called"

"assuming it can read…" I snapped, flouncing out of the itsy-bitsy caravan to go and inspect it for myself.

***

Text to Zoe:

> How u Doing?
> I live in a wilderness.
> Thort u'd like this ad from
> Local paper For Local
> People:
> Sale of Horned & Hill Going
> Ewes & Shearlings & 2nd Sale
> Of Gimmer Lambs.
> Pleez translate: I know u once
> Had a hol in country.

Jim the Plasterer had obviously not read Every Tradesman's Manual on 'How to Irritate Customers' as he not only came, but turned up on time. Even more memorable was that he had a clean BLUE van. We were shocked when he didn't require two cups of black coffee before starting work. He had a 'lad' with him; I wondered if Kim would fancy this one despite his acne, lack of muscle and also, regrettably, lack of hair; for generally Kim fancies anything male on two legs. Jim and the lad were shown my bedroom... well, the empty shell which one day will become a boudoir fit for a teenage Princess (in my dreams!).

"Just needs a skim" Jim, a man of few words, remarked.

At this moment, the strangest thing happened. My mother threw a wobbly. I mean really, really lost the plot! Choking, eyes filling with tears, couldn't string three words together, her face took on the flashing sparks of a massive firework about to explode and land any by-standers in hospital.

"Sorry about this" I, the proxy adult, told Jim gravely. "Are you alright if we leave you to it? Just ask if you need anything..." I was pushing my mother out of the room before her eruption could damage the walls; by now I had realised she was actually laughing, not, unfortunately, choking to death. Jim, poor man, obviously thought I was going out to call the White Coats to deal with the crazy parent and muttered yeah... right... yeah... okay... reassuringly.

Grip of steel (mine) piloted my hysterical mother out of the room, through the kitchen, out of the back door and across the rubbish on the lawn until we were out of ear shot of any of the workmen. My face was a huge question mark.

"Jim the Skim!" she squealed. "Jim the Skim!"

***

Am I losing my touch? Being nasty and punishing my mother for allowing my dear departed father to play away, impregnate his toxic new love and decide he wanted to set up home with her instead of us has been my agenda for the last two months. Going soft? This question engrossed my mind all the way into town where my mother had an appointment with the solicitor to discuss the pony and buy some ready-prepared meals. My brief was to ascertain how I was going to travel daily to my new school. (via cafes and shopping malls or even the library, comes to mind...)

Am I mellowing? She doesn't seem quite as irritating. Crazier, maybe, but perhaps she's learning how to communicate with a bolshy teenage daughter at last. In a flash it came to me that this is probably what happens in every household. Teenage daughter becomes obnoxious, throws hissy fits, perfects the art of tantrum until the parent learns to behave itself and stops being a control freak. Maybe teenagers never 'grow out of it' but actually do such a good job of training parents, that the parents believe the kid has changed whereas it is they who have learnt the Art of Compromise. When I grow up, I shall write a best-selling book on this subject. *This Morning* presenters will review it and I'll sit on their couch and convert parents all over the country. Or not.

Mother has been on holiday from work for two weeks to dismember our orderly lives and move us from a very respectable, much-loved house in town

to the current bomb site we inhabit. Yes, yes, yes, a very small reasonable part of my brain knows that it was inevitable. When he first revealed all his deceptions and infidelities to my mother, my father promised we could keep the family home – and that he would chuck shed loads of money our way. Yeah, right! That was until Toxic Tanya revealed she'd 'forgotten' to take the pill and was carrying my father's child. Suddenly, the family home was to be split in half (financially) so that he could keep the scrawny chick in the manner in which she wished to become accustomed. They would create their own new love nest; Mum and I could sort ourselves out on our half of the proceeds of the house sale.

***

Previous owners of our newly acquired Jasmine Cottage (corny or what!) had replaced the old roof, doors and windows. Sadly, they had bolted out of the country before they ripped out the old (poisonous) lead pipes, updated the central heating system or made sure all the wiring was safe enough for the occupants not to need FrizzEez and soothing balm for burns. Hence our jolly band of workmen.

Our house is not large but neither are we. It will, I am assured, be pretty, comfortable and 'within our budget', whatever that means. My concern is that if my mother dies, like NOW, my father will come and claim it, and probably whisk me away to live with him and his girl-friend and their expected heir. Should that be the case, she of the stick-insect legs and poisonous tongue would probably feed me powdered glass or cocoa laced with arsenic. So I have instructed my mother to discuss with the solicitor the making of a new Will naming me as the sole beneficiary. I'm not a schemer, but you never know, do you? And Toxic Tanya would love to get her hands on anything and everything; she is not to be trusted. I know this because she and I have had several conversations during which she has revealed her true colours. I probably did too! Mutually we loathe and detest! My father can rot; I never want to see him again. He lied, he cheated, he didn't care about causing hurt and then – and this was the worst thing – asked me if I wanted to go and live with him and the Viper, and we could all be a family with my step-sibling. "You cannot be SERIOUS!" I screamed at him and from that moment severed all connection with him. Divorce is pending.

Task one completed: according to instructions I have picked up a load of paint colour charts to choose colours for my bedroom walls and ceiling. No wall-paper as plaster needs time to dry properly, even when only SKIMMED!

Task Two is trickier. At the bus station, I try to persuade a fat woman with orange hair to disclose information about bus times. A closely guarded secret, it can only be cracked by one's ability to decipher pages of small print with numbers and times. This esoteric system requires one to have lived in the area for at least ninety years and know the name of every village and fare stage, according to the tangerine, in a twenty mile vicinity. Alas and alack… it seems I shall not be able to attend school… oh dear!

Are you yawning and muttering 'O get on with it'?

I'm getting there. The next bit is interesting. Feeling a bit guilty because I still didn't know how I was to travel to school, I decided to go to the solicitors and drag my mother to the bus depot to confront Mrs Satsuma. On the way, passing a pet shop, I noticed there were small bags of carrots on a display inside, with a notice saying RABBIT CARROTS. AHA! My Teddy should have a carrot for tea, I vowed.

There were a few people in the shop, and only one lady serving, so I picked up a bag of carrots and wandered around while I waited. On a notice-board advertising dog shampoo, dog trimming, dog walking services, guinea pigs free to a good home, kittens ditto, puppies costing £250 etc. there was a notice advertising a saddlery. Pet shops don't do horses but… I thought a saddler would know what to do about feet the length of curled up oriental slippers. I didn't realise my life was about to change.

I shall, as they say (who is this They?!) cut to the chase. Maggie, the lady behind the counter, and her family, own the pet shop. So huge has been the demand by local horse owners for horse stuff, that this family have recently opened a tack shop in a barn at their livery yard, that's like lodgings for horses… I know this because I've watched cowboy films. Maggie knows a lot about horses. Smug cow – she wouldn't let me buy the carrots because titbits are bad for horses; it makes them ill-mannered, she said.

One paragraph to tell you about Maggie! Wow! Actually I was in the shop for an hour and even shared a pot of tea with her. Eventually my mother rang my mobile as I'd forgotten to meet her as arranged.

Not only did I leave the shop with the number of a farrier (that's a blacksmith to you and me), but lots of information about horses. Not only are titbits bad for them, but they need grooming and from a dusty box under a bench in a store room, Maggie produced several unrecognisable items including a dandy brush, this has coarse bristles for getting mud off My Little Pony, and a headcollar, like a dog collar but far more complicated. This is a gorgeous purple colour and has a lead rope to match. Maggie gave me a crash course in putting it on by using a sweeping brush as the horse's head. If I get it wrong, it will look like my new pony is into bondage!

Best of all, this complex of stables and schools and tack shop, and even a café, is in the next village to Hartwood Green (that's our address. Don't snigger!). I have been invited to go and visit.

From my mother's 'frazzled nerves' point of view, even better is that Maggie has a sister, Beth, who is about my age and she told me which bus to catch to get to my already detested new school. She even offered the absent Beth's services as chaperone but that's awful, isn't it? She'll probably hate me, and I'll feel such a dill if she talks horses and I know Nurthing. All the family, mum, dad, Maggie, Beth, a brother called Leo, two more older sisters who run the tack shop and even, by the sound of it, Uncle Tom Cobbley and all, have horses and ride all the time. She made it sound like fun. They do dressage and go to shows, and Leo jumps things...

Huffing and panting I joined my mother at our meeting place, trying to hide the horsey things in my big shoulder bag.

Praise for colour charts.

Praise for farrier's number.

Praise for finding out about bus to school (even though it will mean Mum driving me up our long lane to the main road each morning).

No praise, though I could see it pleased her, when I requested a bike. I guess I made it sound like I'm planning on exploring the area, and am therefore resigned to living here.

No big deal; just thought I might take up Maggie's offer of going to have a nosey at their place, and maybe have a look in the tack shop.

It DOESN'T MEAN I am settling in. I do not wish to start a new school.

In case she was feeling smug about the bike thing, I sulked all the way home and grumped at her every time she spoke to me.

***

Fitting a headcollar was easier on a sweeping brush than on a live pony who objected to my fingers poking his eyes, the headpiece swinging into his right eye instead of over the top where I could grab it and shifted about so that I had to stand on tiptoe to reach him.

From my description, Maggie described him as a fourteen hand bay cob. Maybe he is; how would I know? I think I forgot to mention the white face and white legs and masses and masses of hair on his lower legs. At last the headcollar was on with the buckle fastened and it didn't look kinky. Ready for anything, buddy boy!

At that point, the project fell flat. What do people do with horses when not riding them? Take them for walks like big dogs? I'd once seen a girl making a big black horse run round her in circles; I'd imagined she was training it to do circus tricks; seemed a sure way of falling down in a dizzy faint to me. Pass on that one, hey Teddy?

Okay, decision time, what shall I do with Teddy today? My mother cannot spend all day shopping; I don't want her to catch me doing anything with a smile on my face; I am not going to forgive her so easily for uprooting and rendering me homeless. In the absence of inspiration, I would lead Teddy round the field to develop a feeling for my space in relation to his space. His feet are massive! Even when the farrier arrives to cut off surplus hoof, they will still be massive. I can imagine that one of his clodhoppers could do permanent damage to my poor girlie skin-and-bone trotters. Eventually I would take him for a walk up the lane, but for now, a traffic free environment felt safer.

He was so pathetically pleased to have a friend that he would have followed me anywhere, I reckon. I stepped forward, Teddy followed. When I stopped, he stopped. Forward again, faster, he speeded up. I wasn't controlling him, he simply mimicked everything I did. When I turned to face him and asked him to move sideways, he responded to a light touch on his side and did a neat side-step, with one back leg crossing in front of the other.

What fun! Temporarily I forgot that he was a horse and I a person who had never touched a horse before. I started doing daft things... running, skidding to a halt, turning sharply one way and immediately the other way, fast run, sudden stop, walk, slow trot. Teddy was so tuned in to what I was doing, he never missed a cue. Through this whole demented workout, he was right next to me, his whiskers tickling my arm, his muzzle almost resting on my shoulder.

What a rotten shame that this lovely critter had been left alone. For a moment I felt his terrible loneliness; I was close to tears. Even cavorting round the field to a silly human's games was better than being alone. How isolated he must have felt, abandoned in this field month after month.

Through the deepest primordial regions of my mind crowded images of horses. Galloping across wind-blown barren landscapes, tails streaming, dust rising; standing erect on craggy vantage points, scenting the wind, scanning the misty distance with long manes blowing in the breeze; grazing safely in cool valley pastures; standing head to tail under trees, tails lazily flicking flies away. Always in herds.

I leaned my forehead against his face, long black forelock tickling my cheek; my hand rested on his neck and he leaned into it. What pain he must have suffered, hungry and alone all this time.

Tears poured from my eyes and trickled down his long face; it looked as if he was crying too.

Chapter 4

Game over! I could get used to this, though! Especially if I could be excused ever going to school again.

I led Teddy to the fence and was about to tie him up when I realised he wouldn't go anywhere. Patiently, he stood and waited, watching me with curiosity. Rocket science it ain't, this grooming lark. Well, come on, common sense tells even non-horsey people like myself, that you brush. It can't be that difficult. Finish with the lie of the coat. It's a breeze.

Except that this pony wanted cuddles and kisses. As I brushed his neck, he pushed his head against me; when I brushed the curved lumpy bit where neck joins body, withers, to those in the know, his top lip grew longer and began to twitch. I was laughing so much at his rapt expression that he nearly knocked me over as he came in for a hefty mutual grooming session; he would, he insisted, use his teeth. At first it was funny being rubbed and pushed and scraped by those big yellow teeth, but after a bit he got so passionate it started to hurt. I called a halt to it before he could break skin.

All his ribs showed through his dull coat. Under his belly, his winter coat had rubbed into tangled matted lumps that hung down like a fringe. Parts of his coat, especially on the shoulders and neck, were showing finer silkier hair where his summer coat was coming through.

Hairy animals… I know about these because we used to have a dog. Judy was the light of my father's eye. He found her, shivering and abandoned in a doorway one wet night and insisted she should come and live with us, providing the RSPCA didn't find her owners. After a few weeks, nobody had claimed her; Mum and I understood why. She was a nasty, mean-spirited, snappy, horrid little terrier. My father was Alpha male to that pooch, he could do no wrong. Mum and I were to take third and fourth place in the pecking order; she would be the Chosen One. Maybe because no-one had ever really adored him like that before, my father thought she was wonderful.

When our Happy Little Family split up so daddy-dear could go and play in the Wendy House with the noxious Tanya, I was asked which parent I wanted to live with. No contest!

Father-dear said "Oh, well, I'll have Judy then".

Made me feel great, wanted, loved… murderous!

Saddest of all, though was that when the venomous new playmate found herself with child, she insisted that Judy should be disposed of. Without a moment's hesitation, my besotted father despatched her to the Great Terrier Heaven in the Sky. Mum remarked "He could have asked us to give her a home rather than killing her". All I could answer was "Maybe he was afraid you'd do a swap and send me to live with him in exchange for the dog!"

I spent about an hour trying to tease out the dangling matted lugs of dead hair, and easing out some of the tangles in Teddy's long unkempt mane. He didn't actually look much better when I'd finished, but that didn't matter because he had enjoyed it so much.

Craig, the farrier, arrived and I held Teddy while he tutted and muttered and said whoever had left a horse in this state should be… well… the various punishments became more elaborate with each successive foot. They started with a mild reprimand from the RSPCA… by the third hoof they were swinging in the wind from a gibbet, eyes bulging. By the fourth and final hoof, my pony was looking remarkably trim and the perpetrators of this terrible crime were being dismembered and fed to hounds of hell with blood dripping from their teeth…

My mother returned from buying taps, plugs, light fittings and emulsion paint in **B&Q**; goody! she paid the farrier. I was rather hoping she would.

Picking her way through discarded packaging and chunks of wood and distorted lengths of copper pipe on the lawn, she glanced over her shoulder and remarked "Wasn't it nice of the blacksmith to give you that headcollar!"

Inner Monster decided to be as awkward as possible about what we should eat for tea; sulking is becoming an art form.

Travelling around in a car doesn't exactly acquaint one with the finer points of agriculture. I've lived all my life in town; fields are part of a green swatch, a patchwork one views at great speed. Hey, we all imagine fields consist entirely of grass which miraculously grows and provides silage or hay, or fattens beef for human consumption. We modern townies know meat doesn't just happen in the supermarket: farmers have hit headlines often enough for us all to know they're getting a rough deal. Supermarkets make vast profits; farmers are forced to try their callused hands at bee-keeping or rare breeds visitor centres or tourist tea rooms.

I have walked on grass; town has its share of parks. The grass is groomed and manicured and mown and sprayed with a green liquid to make it look lush. I never gave any thought to what fields are really like; I imagined they were like park-lawns but with cows.

Even a dope like me recognised that Teddy's field did not fit the stereotype of fields. As he and I performed our unchoreographed dance, it became obvious that all was not well at ground level. Grass, what grass? There was no grass. Tomorrow is Mayday. Spring is going crazy, hedgerows are full of frothy white flowers and hawthorn blossom. Grass is growing; but NOT in my field.

No smoothly groomed lawn here, we have vast bald areas deep in dried horse-droppings. Nettles, docks and thistles, ragwort rosettes, more docks… that's all this poor scrawny pony has to eat. In addition, I later discovered that a) horses don't eat docks, nettles, thistles or (hopefully) ragwort (because it is lethal). b) despite some of the grass growing round the edges of the barren bits, horses won't eat where their own droppings have fallen.

In other words, this pony is on the way to starving to death. No wonder he is eating hedges and chewing wood. Where grass might wish to grow has been totally churned up during the winter as he plodded about in the mud. Spring has neglected to turn up here, knowing the odds are stacked against luscious new growth.

Dawn Chorus… sucks!

D'you know they make tapes and CDs of this racket.

It is DEAFENING.

It hurts my ears.

This is not MUSIC it is a hideous din in stereophonic, quadrophonic, wrap around sound.

It's so intense, it's impossible to pick out individual bird songs; at this level of decibels it sounds more like machinery than sweet little trilled courtship rituals.

The problem here is that while my room is being plastered, I have to share the midget caravan with my mother. The 'beds' are so small, we have to sleep with knees pressed against our chests – foetal position gone mad. In the house, I've obviously been insulated against this daily hullabaloo (love that word!) whereas my parent snores contentedly through it. It is five o'clock and already light. Sleep seems to have fled. I fantasise about procuring an air rifle.

Aaaargh! I'm turning into my mother. Outside, I shiver in my pyjamas and instead of cavorting in the dewy grass I find my feet are pierced by chunks of jagged plaster and sticky cement dust. Hopping and swearing, I fling myself back into the tin-box and wriggle into clothes and sandals. Need ear plugs to live here… or a bird-killing cat…

The parent blows bubbles in her sleep, eyelids flickering slightly. Dreaming, she looks very young, her long dark hair tousled all over the pillow. By day, she orchestrates the Testosterone Brigade, rushes all over the area buying fitments and fittings for our house; she is on first name terms with the men at the builder's merchants; the driver who delivers sand and cement and flagstones and plaster chats her up and stays for a cup of tea. I swear she could win *Mastermind* with her special subject 'Products on Sale at **B&Q**'. When not whipping all the workmen into frenzied action, she spends her time stripping years of paint off wood to reveal the glorious grain beneath. A light, airy, very *blond* house is what my mother is determined to create. She must be exhausted - no wonder she can sleep through the birds' cacophony!

Chapter 5

Early morning in spring has a magical quality. A silvery sun sliding low across the land highlights every dewdrop on every blade of grass until the whole shimmers like a floating rainbow. Every shrub and hedge is decorated with gently swaying gleaming spiders' webs. Dew drips from every surface, catching the light like prism tears.

Already my feet were drenched with dew. The gate was steaming, drips of dew reflecting the sun. I called "Teddy" softly. Busy demolishing a section of hawthorn hedge, the pony heard, his head shot up and he blasted across the field shrieking like an express train.

I was feeling positive as I stroked and chatted to him. For the first time since my father had turned up at our home changed into a totally different person and one whose voice dripped with the slime of Toxic Tanya's thoughts, I had a mission.

That visit was so painful, I think I'd tried to shove it into some deeply hidden cellar in my memory. My father, the shape-shifter, had gone from guilt, remorse and a genuine desire to make things right for Mum and me, to not caring about us at all. He had taken on board Tanya's selfishness and her demands to have all the financial security befitting the mother-to-be of his new child. At first he had said "Of course you and Sahara will keep the house... I'll move out..." This had now been twisted round to "Well... this house is too big for just the two of you... we'll have to sell it and split the proceeds"

"Darling I'll always love you, I'll always be your father, We'll see each other all the time..." now included a casual "'you might have to cut costs... does Sahara need to go to Gymnastics *quite* so often? Most girls of her age get themselves a nice little part-time job to pay for make-up and clothes and..."

The rest of this sentence was lost under my mother's defensive tirade. I hate anger (well, other peoples!) I can't stand hearing people quarrel.

They were no longer restrained and polite, no longer a couple. My parents stood, red-faced and furious, shouting, spitting venom and accusing each other of the most awful deeds of selfishness, cruelty, insensitivity and even, according to my mother, previous adultery.

Trapped in the moment, standing rigid, eyes nearly popping out of my head, hands like misshapen claws, I watched my parents resemble two gladiators prepared to fight to the death. Spit sprayed in all directions; the air crackled with their fury. So sour the atmosphere, so bitter, that in one raucous argument fifteen years of marriage were reduced to an acrid slime.

A high pitched scream startled us all and stopped their vicious insults. A scream so sharp and filled with pain, it hurt my ears, filled my head, and I slammed my hands over my ears to shut it out.

Mouth wide open, a primordial pain found its expression in the only way it could. When I fainted, it was a relief because the screaming stopped.

***

Mission:

    Sort out Teddy's field.

    Find food for him

    Give him as much company as possible

    Improve his condition.

First… I needed to View My Inheritance. My insistence that I would NOT move house, would NOT like living in the country, would NOT treat this bomb-site as home, had rather left me knowing nothing about our domicile (get that!) or, in fact any of the area. That first day when Mum drove me into town, I didn't even know which direction I would be taking to school. I would probably have turned left instead of right at the end of our lane… no knowing where I might have ended up!

Our house is a Victorian cottage with a front door in the middle and a window on either side. Around the front door is a porch with straggly rose bushes trailing over it, they are not in flower yet; Mum thinks they will look wonderful in a few weeks. Upstairs are three windows placed symmetrically directly above the downstairs ones and the front door. A small garden full of builders' rubbish separates the house from the lane and is bordered by a privet hedge.

Now we come to the really exciting part. Imagine this: you are standing in the lane facing our, as yet, rather dull and grotty house. Let your eyes drift upwards, past the porch with its dusty leaves which may, or may not, blaze with flowers one day. Up past the window on the landing, between the two first-floor bedrooms… up… up… Da-daaa! In the roof, two dormer windows. Yes. YES! Two attic rooms.

ALL MINE!

I'm not altogether proud of myself for being so

manipulative but, my poor parent was faced with the choice of me insisting I would rather go and live with… Aunty Jen, Zoe, Kim, Random Foster Parents… or even, yuk, my late-departed father… unless I could have the attic rooms as my penthouse suite. I wheedled, sulked, threw tantrums and almost, but not quite, threw myself on the floor. No terrible two year old could have performed better. Hey, I've had fourteen and a half years to perfect my technique!

Mum agreed, sort of. To save face, she had to impose certain rules. No coffee machine, and NO, I could not have a kitchen. No telly. No loud music. No practising Gymnastics up there.

One room will be my bedroom; I'm still designing it, as the roof slopes down every which way, making awkward corners and few walls high enough for a wardrobe. The other room, bliss! has a toilet and washbasin all boarded in to form a small (incomplete) en-suite. I tried to demand a shower but was beaten back by Mum and Pete the Heat (who is also a plumber) insisting that there wasn't enough head-room for a shower. Whatever that means! I gave in gracefully, acknowledging defeat when it came in the guise of Expert Opinion and one determined parent who had bribed the plumber, I reckon. As well as this cubicle, there is a huge cupboard which utilises the slope of ceiling. Lots of room to stash loads of stuff. The remainder of this room will be my study. Can't WAIT!!!

At this point, I decided to take myself on a tour of The Estate – my inheritance.

Behind the house is a large garden, with a path down the middle of the lawn which is currently covered in rubbish, radiators, tools etc. To one side of this is a garage where all our worldly goods are stored in cardboard boxes, T-chests and suitcases; behind that is a gardening shed and in the corner of the garden there is a large shed full of rubbish.

At the other side of the lawn is the vegetable plot (in your dreams!) with the neatly cut hawthorn hedge dividing it from the field where the pony ekes out a miserable existence. Beyond the vegetable plot is another wooden building which, according to my mother, includes stables, (two in number) and a section for hay, tack etc. Behind all this lot, and you may be forgiven for thinking we have rather a lot of sheds – but bear in mind, the whole site is one-and-a-quarter acres! is an orchard.

A-ha! Grass, trees, grass, grass…

In no time I dressed my pony in his only item of clothing (d'you know when people are selling horses and including rugs and things in the sale, they say 'complete wardrobe'!) and led him through the gate into the orchard. Unclipping him, I was nearly knocked sideways by one crazy steed flinging his back hooves high in the air and showing all the athleticism of a rodeo horse. Bless! He was so excited to have something to eat, he forgot all his manners.

The occupants, until a year ago, of our house have emigrated. That's the official line. Rumour suggests that a variety of scandals - marital, financial and tax related – gave the whole family a hefty push onto trains, planes or boats in the middle of the night; never to return. The estate agent had arranged clearance of the house, and some black-sheep member of the family had acted as agent in the sale until he, too, could make his escape from what might turn out to be several consecutive prison sentences.

Garage, numerous sheds and stables were left full of rubbish.

Lovely! I LOVE rooting. I LOVE treasure hunts!

My pony and I, individually, feel very happy at this moment.

***

Next day…

Various thoughts crowded through my head as I marched my pony, in his smart purple headcollar and matching lead-rope, purposefully along the lane. The first was; how does one avoid ones small delicate skin-and-bone feet being trampled into a mush should this hairy beast decide to grind his hoof and around half a ton of horsemeat on them. Maybe there's no answer to that, except to take great care at all times and never wear flip-flops near a horse.

Then I thought about the willingness of a horse to be lead, pushed around, raced at mighty speeds, made to compete against other horses, pruned, trimmed, clipped, held in captivity and made to leap over high jumps, To say nothing of being squashed into the tiny space-on-wheels of a horse-trailer and trundled all over the countryside, struggling to keep balanced, and bouncing over every grid and pothole, while his ears are being squashed against the roof. It says something about either a) the stupidity of horses to allow all this when they are so much stronger than us or b) the sweetness and forgivingness of their natures.

Other, minor concerns darted in and out of these main pre-occupations. How do horses feel about traffic, for instance? Deliberately I'd brought Teddy out into the lane very early in the morning assuming we would beat the traffic. Should an early-rising farmer appear on a great big green John Deere tractor, would my smart new headcollar be enough to hold my pony. In fact, would I be strong enough to hold my pony? If not, what would he do? Would he run away? How far would he run, in panic? Would he run HOME or in the opposite direction? These are serious problems for a person whose knowledge of horses is ZILCH.

I had sort-of decided to take the view that children and all different species of animals can be trained in roughly the same sort of way. I haven't yet convinced myself that I'm right about this, so don't start watching *This Morning* in the hope that I shall be on their couch (oh! Not HER Again!) when volume two of my work-in-progress is published.

At one point, I did go to dog training classes with my father's nasty, snappy, yappy terrier, in the hope that she might be trained out of biting her owners, or indeed, attacking anything that moved, from cars to cats. Not a success. Sadly, she even snapped at the trainer. I was so embarrassed by my lack of ability to control her in any way, that I left after a few weeks.

Not sure, at this point, whether the principles of dog training are EXACTLY the same as horse training, but I have no other pattern to follow. So when Teddy dragged me across the lane because he had smelt a juicy blade of grass, I spoke sharply to him and insisted he walk to heel. Well, you may laugh, but it seemed to work!

Once he got the idea that our walk was recreational, and nothing to do with stuffing our faces, he trundled along beside me quite sweetly, ears neatly pricked, head up and eyes bright. Everything interested him, from bits of rubbish in the hedges to birds flitting across our path. I guess if you've spent a year in solitary confinement, the world will seem an interesting place and what once was familiar will have changed in subtle ways.

I was feeling very pleased with myself because I had made a start on The Mission: he had a fairly full stomach and had been groomed, played with and now exercised. In the period where he was fattening his face, I had cleared the litter and rubbish, including a tyre and old oil drums out of his paddock in phase one of the Great Clean Up.

When my phone rang, he skittered sideways and I laughed at him. It was a text from Kim:

> That gorjus Mike asked for
> My phone number. I cd die!

For a surreal moment I felt totally detached from my body; Kim and her boyfriends, Zoe, the whole Gymnastics thing… even my old school… felt like things that had happened in a film or a book.

Somehow in the past week, I'd shifted into another life.

I pressed Reply, then:

> Good 4 u.
> Out for walk with my pony.
> Fantastic morning.

As I pressed Send, I burst into tears. I didn't know who I was any more.

Long hair loose and gently blowing in the breeze, my mother was sitting on the step of the mini-caravan, both hands clasped loosely round a cup of coffee. Teddy and I had come round the corner quietly, walking on the grass, and she hadn't heard us.

How could my father have left her for that insipid featureless stick-insect, I wondered. Even though she irritated me to the point of insanity, even I could see that she was beautiful, bright, feisty, sensitive, clever and artistic. Who would want long skinny legs and a whiney voice instead of that? Well, my father, obviously!

Glancing up, she caught sight of us and a huge smile crossed her face. This is how horrible I am: immediately, I was bad-tempered and rude. "Don't look so bloomin' smug" I snapped "this doesn't mean that I am going to live here, enjoy living here, or ever forgive you for dragging me away from all the stuff I wanted in my life"

"Oh" was all she said, the smile replaced by hurt and bewilderment.

"I only took the stupid horse out for a walk because I feel sorry for him" I shouted "and because, like me, he's being forced to live a life he hates"

With that, I jerked the lead rope and startled Teddy into a few steps of trot.

"I didn't say anything… " she called softly.

"No. Well, don't" I snarled.

Teddy stopped dead, slightly behind me, and I walked on without him for a few steps. When I was brought to a halt, I turned and shouted "Come on, you" turning his head, he looked directly at my mother, then at me.

"Come on" I whispered gently, wanting to get away from my mother's hurt expression. Sticking out his muzzle, he pushed my upper arm delicately… just a touch… then walked with me.

I don't speak Horse. I don't know what they understand, what they think… but I felt as though I had been repri-manded. Yes, okay, I know this was just my inner voices tell-ing me I'd behaved badly; yeah, yeah… it's called guilty conscience. I KNOW this… but…

Grass had been provided; he'd had an interesting walk; now Teddy stood in the silvery sun as midges tested the air around him and fences steamed. I surveyed the mammoth task of cleaning up his field. This was going to be a huge challenge. For a moment, I wished Zoe could be here to laugh with me about it – or even help me. I sent her a text:

> Take day off school
> & hitch a lift. Need yr help
> shifting several tons of shit.

Later, her answer came:

> as usual, u r deep in it
> Shift it yrself.
> Miss u

Borrowing a wheelbarrow I found amongst the builders' debris on the lawn, I sneaked off with it before the 'lads' arrived. I found a shovel and a rake in the gardening shed. Maybe they belonged to us, maybe not. So much junk had been left behind by the previous owners, I no longer knew what was ours. And that included a pony!

Occasionally Teddy wandered over to blow warm air on me as I laboured. Sometimes he followed me to the gate and tried to squeeze through it with me as I trundled my stinking load to the midden. His company was good; I could take a break on the pretext of talking to him.

In some ways it was weird. For years I had trained and exercised and honed my body, strengthening it for Gymnastics. From the day my father had so belittled my efforts, I'd lost heart. Though I still trained and attended every session, my heart wasn't in it. Psychologically I was already leaving it behind, knowing that our move to the country was imminent. I had always believed it was the one thing in life I was truly passionate about, but gradually I started to understand it had been an obsession. Not real love, but a habit, an addiction.

By the time we had moved to our country building site, I was going through withdrawal symptoms; I'd lost the hunger for success, but I'd also lost some part of myself.

All those years, I had revelled in the hardness of my body, lean, toned, not a pinch of excess fat anywhere. Now… phew!

Barrow sixteen. I was exhausted!

Barrow seventeen felt as though my arms were dropping off.

Barrow eighteen…

How does she DO that…? My mother appeared at the field gate carrying a tray. Teddy got to her first and I heard her laugh as she pushed him away.

"Breakfast!" she called gaily. WHY does she forgive me. How CAN she love my Inner Monster when it hurts her so?

The tray was a peace offering. I wandered over and said "Thanks" though it sounded sullen.

"You missed breakfast" she commented.

"Hmmm. Wanted to make a start on this… it's so disgusting… " I bit into a piece of jammy toast. Wow! Best piece of toast I've ever eaten.

"D'you want some help?" she asked casually.

"Dunno…" *yes yes yes* "I guess so… if you've nothing better to do" I shrugged.

"I have to go into work for an hour or so… and to **B&Q**… and I thought I'd call at some of the houses up the lane and see if anybody knows anything about the pony… but I could give you a hand for a while – if you want"

"That would be good" I met her eyes "Soz, Mum"

"I know" she said, picking up the shovel and pushing it firmly into the deep mound of dried and compacted droppings.

"Sometimes…" she said as she wobbled past me with a laden barrow "we take out our anger on the wrong people…" pausing to open the gate, as I wiped my sticky hands on my jeans "but maybe that's better than letting it all pile up inside us…" she swept her hand towards the depth of dung "like that stuff…"

"Mum… I am sorry…"

"I know. Hey… it will pass" and she struggled towards the midden to dump another load.

Chapter 6

Wow! It's busy in the country.

No time to get bored; it's really hectic.

Here's what happened today – in between idiot workmen asking "do you know where…? have you got…? are there any…? where's your mum…? in all sorts of combinations. Fortunately, there's a stock answer to any possible question they might ask: the tone of voice is the key: "Dunno!"

Jim not only finished skimming the walls in my two rooms (YES!!!) but also started on my mother's bedroom. That's good, by the way, because it means two things, a) I won't feel guilty when I wallow in my two rooms, and sleep in a proper bed etc. and b) it will reduce any risk of her begging to be allowed to sleep in one of my rooms until hers is ready.

Not only that, but Electric Eric is busy gluing electric sockets and light switches to the wall, and finishing the wiring for lights. So exciting! I shall soon have a room.

Not just any room, though – a room with radiators!

It is all HAPPENING! Pete the Heat is also in there, sorting out the central heating. (Okay… I know it won't be working until the system is finished all over the house… but in a day or two my rooms will look like rooms and I will be allowed to start chucking paint at the walls and ceiling!)

Because a major decorating job is imminent, there's more urgency about sorting out Teddy's field, so today I've shifted hundreds of millions of barrow loads of muck. Literally. Well (and I've been counting) sixty-two loads, that includes the ones my mother wheeled before departing for her second home – **B&Q**.

Everything becomes more desperate with the threat of school hanging over me. As I shovel manure and wheel barrows, I work on a project to convince my mother and the education authorities that my education will be better served in learning practical skills than sitting bored out of my head in a fusty classroom among strangers. Consider this, I say to an unseen audience… if I stay at home I shall be learning essential skills in animal husbandry, including the care of an equine… painting, carpentry, horticulture, land management… people skills (does grunting 'Dunno' at frequent intervals constitute personnel interaction?)

I still haven't found time to have a good rummage in our many outbuildings. The only thing I did was push my way through all the spiders' webs (ugh) and dust in the stable to uncover a huge pile of hay bales. (Errr….what's a huge pile? I haven't a clue how much a horse eats. There are about 15 bales; is this good?) I cut the string on one of the bales and chucked a section of slightly dusty hay over the fence to Teddy. He didn't move until he had eaten every last bit of it. (Does that mean he was hungry? Duh… joke!)

My honourable parent returned from pillaging and looting to tell me she had, as well as popping into work, no doubt to catch her staff up to no good in her absence! and, of course, going to **B&Q** for her daily fix, she had done the genteel 'calling on neighbours to introduce herself' bit. Anti-climax or what? They were all either out or so secure behind their remote-controlled five metre high designer gates she was unable to attract their attention. AND... here's the good stuff! The farmer who owns the land next to ours was not only at home, but insisted on Mum going into their big farmhouse kitchen (what else?) for a cup of tea, the lowdown on everyone else who lives (handsomely, most of them) on the lane... and

Ta-daa! Teddy.

Teddy IS called Teddy. Whew! What if he'd been a girl? Actually I knew he was a boy because if you bend down and look under the belly... that's where horses keep their boy-bits! A girl used to live in our house and she rode him for a while but then seemed to lose interest. He told my mum a lot of stuff that she wasn't revealing to me because it's 'adult' and according to her, probably untrue and libellous.

When they, for various unsavoury reasons, did a 'moon-light flit' Teddy was left behind. The happy farmer and his wife, called Ned and Shirley, had kept an eye on my hapless pony and thrown him hay in winter and when the field looked very bare. "If they'd left a wheelbarrow" Ned said to Mum "you wouldn't have any problem in keeping it and using it, would you? Keep the pony... your girl (!) can ride it... it's yours... view it as fixtures and fittings."

"Well" Shirley had butted in "they certainly won't be coming back for it"

"What d'ya think?" Mum asked casually, but I noticed an alert glint in her eye.

"Mmmmm" I commented.

"What does that mean?" behind her smile lurked irritation.

"Could do. He could stay here, I s'pose" shrugging my shoulders.

"D'you think you might... er... well... one day... want to learn to ride?" she asked.

My next book (watch for me AGAIN on Richard and

Judy) is probably going to be entitled The Art of Grunting, It's a wonderful form of communication, a bit like barbed wire is a wonderful form of fencing. Nasty, but effective. Says BEWARE. Some of the lads at school were absolutely brilliant. They could stare at their feet, grunt… and we ran a mile. You don't mess with anyone who grunts as well as that. It takes practise… diligent practise, and patience. Probably even some work in front of a mirror.

Comparatively, I'm a total novice. Trouble is, you see, I don't practise. Deep down inside, a part of me wants to communicate with words and eye contact, I guess I'll never make it as a Grunter; but my mother doesn't know that… she isn't aware of the full impact of a really effective delivery from an expert. So, like a parent who thinks their wooden, tone deaf offspring has a 'luvly voice' my parent is fooled by my immature, unrehearsed grunts.

The foregoing was a link, as they say in television. A link to the next event of that particularly busy day - the unexpected arrival of Maggie (remember – I told you about her in the pet shop) and her younger sister Beth.

Grunting was the order of the day. Maggie breezily chatted to me and Beth and we both responded to her, but grunted at each other. I expect she hated me as much as I loathed her. I suppose she had been dragged kicking and screaming into the red Defender and driven down our lane in (humiliation upon humiliation) her school uniform. She looked as uneasy in it as I would feel in (aaargh) a few days time.

Which was why Maggie had come calling. She had remembered I was due to start school soon and offered me a lift. "I'm passing the end of the lane… it's only a tiny detour… and I'm dropping Beth at the school gates… it's as easy to take two as one…"

The unthinkable alternative was my fond parent, not only running me to the school gates, but insisting on marching me into the school and introducing me to the Head Teacher or whoever would be responsible for my welfare... I'd be lucky to escape her trying to hold my hand... Eeeekkkk!

So I said yes to Maggie, trying to ignore Beth's face of thunder. I got her... understood exactly how gross it would be for her being stuck with the new girl... maybe having to mentor me and show me the toilets and where the canteen was... I would have hated it, too.

My mother had unstuck herself from the paint removing gunk by this time and bustled out to offer cups of tea and a very dirty handshake. Our first visitors! her sparkling eyes said to me. Yeah, right!

"Do you have a pony, Beth?" (Oh, go AWAY, mother!)

 Beth responded with a couple of grunts and Maggie translated "We have loads of horses on the yard, Beth has her own Working Hunter Pony and helps us with breaking and schooling any ponies that come in. It's great to have a capable smallish rider on hand"

Oh wow. Bad move! Now Mum is going to have to chuck something in there about how brilliant I am at Gymnastics. It's impossible for a parent to hear praise without matching it.

Trying to break up the party I muttered "D'you want to come and see Teddy?" and Beth grunted appreciation. So off we went.

Not surprisingly, once out of adult ambience (and hearing) we could have a conversation using normal everyday tones. And words!

When she enthused "Oh! He's gorgeous! I bet he has a coat like a teddy bear in winter... what a sweetie!" I blushed with pleasure. At that moment, I vowed to be her friend forever.

"You won't have to look after me at school" I muttered – the best gift I could think of.

"Don't mind, really" she smiled.

By the time we returned to the interfering sister and the interfering parent, Beth and I had come to an unspoken agreement. When we were told that I was to be entertained by Beth at their place on Sunday (don't bother ASKING us, will you?) we sort-of rolled our eyes at each other and shrugged.

"How lovely for you to have a friend at school" my mother gushed as their red Land Rover bucketed away up the lane (at least she didn't say LITTLE friend!).

"Uugghh" I grunted, scuffing my toe against the gravel path.

"Well, at least you'll know someone" she wheedled.

"Urrrggh"

Pulling a funny face, she returned to her paint removing.
PROBLEM!

If I'm offered a ride, what do I do? Too early in a friendship, or whatever it is, to reveal my total incompetence as a keeper of a horse (even though Maggie will have told her I know Nurthing). I will probably look stupid on a horse, but I don't want her to know that. She's probably got loads of brilliant friends who are 'capable smallish riders' and will laugh like drains when they know I have a pony I can't ride.

Cancel! That's the easy thing to do.

Or, go wearing a skirt. I never wear skirts except for school. In fact, I don't even have a non-school one – much to my mother's disgust!)

Break a leg…

An arm…

Or… learn to ride. (In two days, I hear you snort?! Learn to RIDE in two days… Yeah! Right on!)

My mother chose my moment of indecision, as I chewed

my finger-nails down to the knuckle to drift out of the house on her way to collect a take-away for tea. Teddy was chilled, having recently had his ration of one hour's grazing in the orchard. Watching my mother's dusty black Golf drive away, I came to a decision.

After all, how difficult can it be…?

Nervously, I retrieved the pink baler twine I'd cut from the bale of hay and knotted one end of it to the metal part on one side of the headcollar, and the other end to the other side. I know, I know! Normal riders use a bridle and metal bit, but I hadn't got one and time was short. My makeshift reins were not elegant, but they would have to do. I trusted my chilled pony to behave like a true gentleman.

As I fitted his headcollar, I told him the score and asked forgiveness in advance for any mistakes I might make. Hey, I've watched dressage riders on telly – it doesn't LOOK all that difficult. Forgot to mention, proper riders also use a saddle. A saddle, I realised, provides a stirrup in which to place foot and leap neatly onto horse's back. I could, you understand, vault on. I've been leaping on and off horses for years, but generally they're pretty immobile and don't lash out with their hind legs if you get it wrong.

Fetching the stepladder from beside the back door, I placed it next to Teddy's shoulder and, wobbling a little, climbed up. Not sure what was happening, Teddy whizzed round to have a look, leaving me atop the ladder with a fist-ful of pink baler twine, and a certain loss of dignity.

Pushing the pony sideways against the hedge, I dragged the ladder into place again, wobbled up it, and this time managed to get a leg across his neck before he moved forward and left me muttering Very Strong Language whilst balancing on one leg.

Third time lucky. As I teetered precariously on the ladder

and stretched a leg towards his back, I snapped "STAND!" Shocked, he stood stock still and allowed me to settle onto his back. Ooookkkkaaaayyyy.

Wide… slippery… My legs dangled down his sides and my wellies felt as though they would slip off… but… hey! I was on a horse. Gathering up my flimsy pink reins, I tested how effective they would be should I need to stop him. Not at all. They would, I had to admit to myself, be totally useless. Just have to hope I won't need to stop him, I told myself shakily.

Surveying the world from his back, I felt quite smug. Through his warm back I could feel the minute movements of his body… blood circulating, a pulse, heart, liver, kidneys functioning. Privileged to feel his life teeming beneath me, I reached forward and stroked his neck. Only a few days previously, his coat felt dull and lank. Now it felt more silky and smooth with all the grooming I'd done.

My pony!

I have a pony!

When I'd sat there for a while, with Teddy dozing beneath me, I wondered how it would feel to sit on him as he – like… er, well - moved.

Right. Small problem! How d'you get a sleepy horse to move?

I shook my pink stringy reins but he didn't seem to notice them.

This CANNOT be difficult. People ride horses all the time. I tried clucking noises and more shaking of the string. Nothing happened.

From some deep, long-buried memory I heard two girls in the canteen at school talking 'ponies' over lunch. One had obviously been competing… clear rounds and times and heights of jumps were mentioned, but I wasn't registering any of it. "I was coming up to the last... I knew I'd done a wicked time... and he tried to put in a stop. I kicked him so hard, he absolutely flew it... and..."

The only reason I gave this conversation any importance at the time was because of the 'kicked him so hard' bit. My imagination took off, and I visualised her leaping from his back and rushing at him to kick his shins. It took me a while to work out exactly how she must have kicked him.

"Teddy... if you don't budge, I'm afraid I'm going to kick you" I told him apologetically. Nothing happened. I jiggled my weight into balance on his back, took both legs way out to the sides and slammed them against him.

! ! ! ! !

Maybe I need to explain several things here.

Firstly, I am a gymnast; I have very, very strong legs.

Teddy had not been ridden, as far as I knew, for about a year so had probably forgotten that people on his back are likely to crush all the air out of his lungs with legs like vices.

From the outside the scene would have looked like a Thelwell cartoon.

From my angle... well, to put it mildly, it was a bit of a shock.

Remember, I'm a gymnast. In all the years I've been training, I've not only built strength, but learned to control all the bits and appendages of my body. At all times I have to be aware of the shapes my limbs are making, whether toes are pointed, neat and elegant...

HA!

From a daydream state, my pony was galvanized into something resembling a Whirling Dervish. When I say 'he took off' I mean He Took Off! One minute I was sitting astride his warm back and the next... well...

What word can describe it? Airborne, perhaps. In flight.

Flying, diving…

Bear in mind that, as a gymnast, I have performed perfect somersaults, handstands, walk-overs, pirouettes, vaults, double-piked Sukaharas… you get the gist?

Well, this removal of self from pony was all of those rolled into one.

One minute, smugly perched on his back, the next, totally without grace, elegance or control, smashing into a hawthorn hedge and landing in a very clumsy heap on the grass while his hairy bottom raced across the field as if all the hounds of Hell were snapping at his heels.

OUCH!

As I picked thorns out of my flesh, and did a mental inspection of my various limbs and appendages, seeking fractures, bruises or torn ligaments, Teddy wandered casually back across the paddock, snorting slightly (Blushing, even?) and blew warm air on my embarrassed face. From my position on the hard soil, he looked gigantic, hairy and…

adorable!

Back to the drawing-board!

Maybe I was a tad strong there. I really don't want to break my head. This time… gently, gently.

Teddy stood quietly while I climbed the ladder again. One ear was twitching back towards me, no doubt preparing himself for another crashing blow to the ribs. Wriggling as little as possible, I settled myself astride his warm back, and once more viewed my inheritance from this vantage point.

Yes, there were dozens of questions plaguing my mind: do I really want to get hurt? Is this going to be worth it? Is it possible to teach myself to ride in three days? Am I being a total buff-head in thinking I can do this?

Taking a deep breath, I pushed my legs very gently against Teddy's sides.

YES!

With no fuss he stepped forward. I am a RIDER! I can do this! Eezy-peezy!

Three steps later, I found myself in serious difficulties and the elation subsided. Horses' bums wobble as they walk. Did you know that?

It's amazing how much movement there is under a rider. As each hind leg steps forward, the whole body rocks... then the other leg swings forward and the one is hurled the other way. Without a saddle, this is a serious issue.

Teddy kept walking, so I shifted my bottom on his back so that I was properly balanced. He didn't seem to notice that I was slithering about, so maybe that's how it always feels to him.

Half-way down the field, it occurred to me that I should be doing more than sliding about up there – steering, for example. Taking a firmer hold on my pink stringy reins, I pulled to the right. Teddy turned his head slightly but continued in a straight line along the hedge.

This could become embarrassing, I thought, having no desire to be found later embedded in a hawthorn hedge. I tried again, this time, pulling gently on the rein and turning my body to the right. This pushed my right leg against his shoulder, and the left leg farther back. Weird or what! he turned!

No bucking displays, no wheelies, no standing on hind legs and waving front legs in the air, my pony was being very patient with me. As my confidence increased, I relaxed more. As I relaxed more, my bottom seemed to sink deeper into his back and I felt secure.

Another interesting thing was that as I relaxed, Teddy's head dropped lower. At first, his ears were nearly up my nostrils and his spine felt really tight. As we got used to each other, it all felt easier and less bumpy.

Concentrating very hard, I walked him forward a few steps, then asked for a left turn, focussing on turning my head and shoulder slightly to the left and pressing my left leg against him so that it felt as though I was wrapping him round my left leg.

YES!

Right angled corners were hard, because they unseated me. A bare back is slippery. One minute I was in place; the next I was sliding off to one side or the other. Teddy's ears told me when I was unsettling him.

You are probably screaming at the page 'But you can't STOP him, you dork. It's no good being able to do right turns and left turns if you can't STOP!'

I hear you! It's exactly what my own voice was screaming inside my head.

Using my legs, I sort-of nudged the pony onto a circle, thinking that would give me a continuous loop in which to devise a system for halting. Not quite like a bike without brakes… I couldn't scrape my foot along the ground to stop him. Using the leg on the inside of the circle against him, and with a pull on the rein, I managed to keep him moving in a rather lumpy shape, more potato than circle. If I pulled very hard on the string, he ducked his head about. Shouting Woah! didn't help. The situation wasn't worrying enough for me to bale out.

Frustrated, I gave a sigh like a huge puff of air and my bottom sagged more onto his back. He stopped. Uh?

Gently nudging him forward again into walk, I tried again, imagining it was a fluke.

Pony walked forward, I fingered the reins, breathed out, straightened my back. Pony stopped.

Uh?   UH?   UH?

This was the moment when it all went pear-shaped.

I heard a car on the lane and recognised the very dusty roof of my mother's black Golf.

So? you may ask.

Mothers. You know how they can be, If mine saw me involving myself in riding (if that's what one can call it) she would smirk in that nauseating way; perhaps even say "See... I told you it would be fun living in the country"

Aaargh. I needed to be out of there. And quick!

Poor Teddy. One moment I was, I believe, learning how brakes are applied when astride a horse. The next, forgetting I was nearly two metres above the ground, I swung my leg over his neck in an attempt at a quick dismount.

Dismount. That word has many connotations for me. In Gymnastics, a Dismount is the graceful, controlled way one finishes an exercise and makes contact with the ground again. Often this involves very elaborate twists and turns, like somersaults, back-flips, handstands or cartwheels. Balanced and graceful, the culmination is the Landing which must be solid, controlled and with both feet firmly planted exactly where required.

Hmmm! Exactly the opposite of my dismount then!

Poor Teddy, never having been kicked on the head by his rider before, put his head between his knees and did a fair imitation of some of the gymnastic moves I've been describing to you. Graceful he was not; determined, yes.

Meanwhile me, his hapless rider, found myself performing previously unknown gymnastic moves which involved a certain amount of grabbing at air, squealing and total loss of control.

Once more, I found myself covered in dust with thorns sticking out of my flesh, and a nettle rash already blotching my skin.

"Hiya! Having a rest?" my mother's head appeared over

the gate as I crawled on all fours to a hiding place under the hedge.

"Mmm… no… just er…" I gritted my teeth.

Teddy the traitor, hearing her voice, rushed to the gate to say hello. Of course, he was still wearing his pink string reins, but they were dangling over one ear.

"Oh" said my mother cheerily "that colour really suits you, Teddy"

Carefully I hauled myself upright, wincing as every bone in my body screamed 'fracture!' Well… maybe 'bruise!'

Sometimes my parent deserves a Gold Star for effort. Instead of asking why my teeth were gritted and my smile was a rictus of pain she said "Phew… it was busy in **B&Q** today." then over her shoulder called "Tea in ten minutes." leaving me yelping with pain as I limped to my unrepentant pony to retrieve his 'wardrobe', the pink reins.

Chapter 7

Delighted to be going to Maggie and Beth's yard – if only to take my mind off the feeling of dread when I thought of New School the week after next – I made an effort to be charming to my mum and didn't even twiddle the knobs of the radio on our way there.

Interesting here: when I didn't fiddle with the radio, Mum became quite jittery. I guess she's so used to me messing with it - just to annoy her - when I didn't, she feared something worse. In the end, quite agitated, she switched on the radio herself. Even more amusing – when it was tuned into her favourite Classic FM, she changed it to one with pop music. I'm sure there is some very important lesson on 'How to Manipulate People' embedded in this little scenario. Shall give this some thought… it may well provide a follow-up volume to 'Every Teenager's Guide to Stropping'.

In my dreams, I'd imagined Oak Tree Stables would be a haven of tranquillity, with lots of horses' heads looking out over stable doors, or plump ponies standing contentedly under trees in a paddock. Yeah! Right! Not only was it sheeting rain, but the chaos in the yard almost made me leap back into the car and beg to be ferried home.

Mud, everywhere.

Ponies, everywhere.

Kids, everywhere.

Perhaps because of the rain, all the livery horses were sheltering in stables or under the stable canopies, or ducking into the indoor school for shelter.

In the car park, a pony was being unloaded from a huge purple horse-box. Leading the rugged, bandaged, booted bay down the ramp was Beth. Her dad followed behind with a haynet, grooming box, jacket and bags.

"There you go" Mum pointed towards Beth, revved the engine and drove away in a splatter of gravel and a tsunami of puddle-water. Standing in the pouring rain, I felt totally useless. Obviously this was a bad time; everybody looked grumpy; I would be in the way. Nevertheless, I stood my ground, even though I felt like rugby tackling my mum's car and being dragged home, if necessary, clinging to the rear bumper.

Beth's smile was friendly enough. "It's been horrendous" she called "I've been to a hunter trial... it was a mud-bath... Zeb is FILTHY... I'll have to wash his legs... can you help Dad unload the wagon? sorry I wasn't here when you arrived... " and disappeared with the pony into the stable block.

"Er... I'm Sara... I said to her dad "Can I carry something?"

"Beth told me you'd be here... she's driven me mad nagging about getting back in time to meet you... bring the tack, will you..."

Feeling inadequate and rather lost, I went up the steep ramp into the horse-box. Cor! What a dream! It was so posh... it even had a kitchen with cupboards and proper spaces with racks for saddles and bridles. Oh no! I'm turning into my mother... the thought in my head was 'this must have cost nearly as much as our house!' With the bridle was a really pretty red rosette with 1st printed on it in gold. Am

I in the company of greatness? I wondered. She's going to think I'm such a dork. She's won a first prize.

I wanted to go home.

Eventually I struggled back down the ramp loaded with an assortment of tack and rugs, and the rosette.

Maggie was crossing the yard "There you are... I'm really sorry about this... there was a huge delay... they had to stop all the horses on the course when a girl came off and they rang for the Air Ambulance. Can you imagine how awful that was... horses were freaking all over the course... it was a wonder there weren't MORE injuries because of the helicopter... so it was ages before they opened the course and restarted... D'you want a brew or anything... we've just got to see to Zeb... he needs washing and feeding... and I bet his tack is disgusting so Beth will want to clean that..."

Phew! Maggie can talk for England! At least it spared me having to make conversation as I followed her to where Beth was washing mud off her pony's legs. Over her shoulder, Maggie was still wittering on... giving me a brief history of every pony we passed, greeting people, shouting at some kids for 'fooling about' around the stables...

Standing in the doorway of the stable, I watched Beth and Maggie busy themselves making Zebedee comfortable. About as big as Teddy, he wasn't as chunky, and he had a very pretty face with a bright curious expression. I wanted to ask what Hunter Trials were about, but didn't want to appear ignorant. I also wanted to know what they were doing... why wash his legs... how did they know what to feed him... was it easy to win a red rosette... Beth had never even smiled when I held it out to her; had it been mine, I'd have been wearing it pinned to my fleece or something. Later I saw her collection of rosettes and realised why another one wasn't a big deal!

All afternoon, I was being introduced to different members of Beth's family. I didn't even try to remember their names. There were her mother and father, then a variety of sisters, their partners, husbands and fiancés, and a couple of brothers. Sundays were gathering of the tribe occasions, her dad told me as I struggled after him through mud and heavy rain to muck out the horsebox which was then parked away round the back of the barn.

Maggie, who after all had been responsible for inviting me, insisted on looking after me and introducing me to people – not only family, but owners who had horses on livery at the yard, and even some of the kids with ponies stabled there. It seemed noisy, hectic and great fun.

Various sisters nagged at Beth to go and have a hot bath. When the event was halted due to a rider needing the Air Ambulance, she had been out 'in the sticks' (as she put it) on Zebedee; it was absolutely pissing down and her riding jacket was so wet, they could wring water out of it. All the time she was making her pony comfortable and trying to be friendly to me, her teeth were rattling with cold. "GO!" I insisted at last "go and have a bath and get warm. I'll be fine… I'll just watch what's going on in the indoor school"

"Are you SURE?" Beth asked.

"Just GO!" I ordered. Later I realised that was a turning point in our relationship; we were being open with each other. Not true friends, yet, maybe… but easier together.

Maggie brought two mugs of tea out and led the way into the 'viewing gallery' of the school. It was rudimentary. The seating was wooden planks fixed onto concrete plinths; no heating; no cushions.

"Sorry it's a bit basic" Maggie laughed. "I suppose we've got used to it"

"It's fine" I assured her "it's dry!"

If you imagine some influential figure had stood up and shouted "LET'S HAVE A WILD RUMPUS!" you may have an idea of the frenzy before us.

"It's because it's wet" Maggie explained "Normally, most of these kids meet up on a Sunday and go off for a picnic ride, or a hack... or even go to a show somewhere."

"It's really Enid Blyton, isn't it?"

Maggie threw back her head and roared with laughter.

"Not sure about that... but I get your point... more Ruby Ferguson or Monica Edwards maybe"

"Never heard of them" I leaned back as a pony cantered past and splattered us with the soft mix of sand and rubber-shred that formed the surface of the school.

Whizzing round the school in a variety of directions and speeds, including gallop, were about six kids on ponies... no... seven... It was manic.

"They're supposed to be schooling their ponies" Maggie explained "but most of them haven't a clue what that means" (me neither!) "and of course they razz each other up... any minute, one of them will suggest jumping and these poor ponies will be hammered over ridiculously high jumps all afternoon unless one of us puts a stop to it"

"And will you?" I asked, sipping my tea.

"Of course... I don't care a toss about the kids... but I DO care about the ponies. They don't MEAN to be hard on them... they just want to have fun..."

One of the older sisters popped her head round the doorway and shouted "PHONE, Maggie!"

"be back in a sec" Maggie was apologetic.

"It's okay" I said "I'm enjoying watching them" and actually enjoyed it more when Maggie went and I could scrutinise their riding.

Smug-face, me. Sitting in judgement when I've only ridden once, in walk, bareback and without a bridle! All the years I've trained in Gymnastics have involved sharing apparatus, space, coaches. We all spent much of every training session sitting waiting for our turn to come round… watching, analysing, learning from other people's mistakes. Analysis has always been an important part of development as an athlete. Left to myself, it was an automatic reaction to assess what was going on before me.

Hey! I'm not saying I could do it right, but even as a non-horse person it became obvious when a pony was unhappy or refusing to do something. Swishing tails and mean expressions and an unwillingness to go forward are all screaming one thing. I started to read body language; when unhappy, the horses would sort of hollow their backs and stick their noses in the air. Watch! in that position, movement becomes stilted… the back legs can't work properly. I'd felt that with Teddy in certain moments, and it was fascinating to watch it in a detached way.

Sometimes people say there is no such thing as a bad dog – only a bad owner.

I was witnessing that with horses. Even to a total novice like myself, it was obvious that most of what went wrong was due to the rider, not the horse.

Gradually I started to recognise individual ponies from the scrum and to pick out where their problems originated. One rider was banging down so hard on the poor animal's back, it must have been in agony. A small girl with pink scrunchies in her hair, tugged the reins every time her pony did anything… I mean anything! She was stiff and rigid and terrified; so she used the reins randomly, see-sawing them in the poor animal's mouth. Then the pony would start running backwards to avoid the snatching bit… and the child would tug some more. How could she NOT realise that when she released the vicious pressure on the bit, the pony moved forward quite sweetly. Why did none of the other kids point this out to her? Why have her parents not realised? It's so obvious.

"Do these kids have lessons?" I demanded as Maggie plonked herself down beside me.

"Yup. Most of them do. And we all try to get through to them…" She smiled at me "It's scary, isn't it?!"

"Does it have to be so violent?"

"Strong word!" she shuddered. "Some of it is about being scared, especially in this crazy environment. See her…" she pointed to a pale, blonde girl on a pale blonde pony "she rides really well when she's on her own… look at her now, though… her bottom is hardly on the saddle… she's hanging onto the reins for support and probably wants to cry for her mummy. She just shouldn't get involved with this lot… they josh each other on and show off… the trouble is, that's what a lot of the stuff connected with riding is about!"

"I don't like it much then" I said.

"I came to ask you if you want to come and help me clean Beth's tack. She'll be out soon. Maybe we can find a pony for you to ride…"

"In this" I shuddered "NO thanks!"

Wanting to learn, I watched closely as Maggie pulled the bridle apart. So many straps and buckles! I thought I would never know how to put it all back together.

I had confessed to never having cleaned tack, so Maggie didn't expect much of me. "Take the leathers and girth off the saddle, and throw the numnah over there for washing" she instructed. (Oh crikey… what's a numnah? Well, the only thing that could be washed was the saddle cloth thingy, so I threw that to one side and she didn't yell 'What d'you do that for?') I managed to slide the stirrup leathers off the bars, unbuckled them and slipped the stirrups off. Ha! Expert already!

Following Maggie's example, and heeding her warning not to use too much water... sponge only just damp! I washed and soaped and buffed and felt very smug.

Meanwhile, like a conjurer, she had magicked the mess of straps back into a gleaming bridle.

We had just finished when Beth reappeared, damp and smelling of soap and shampoo. "Sorry I've been such a lousy hostess" she said.

"Lousy hostess, lousy sister, lousy rider... what's new?" Maggie laughed.

"And you timed the tack cleaning just right" I told her, expertly (well, expertly for a very first attempt) slipping stirrups back onto leathers and attaching them to the saddle.

"Come on" she nodded her head at me "I'm taking you into the shop. We only opened six weeks ago... it's fantastic... I still love it... the smell of leather... ahhhh!"

Outside, it had stopped raining and a feeble sun was filtering through clouds. I thought of Teddy in his field, drenched to the skin and hungry... but that was the way it had been for him for (at a guess) about a year.

"Are horses alright left out in fields in this weather?" I asked as we picked our way through puddles towards the huge barn housing the tack shop.

"They have plenty of grease in their coats; they find shelter; in the wild, they live out in all weathers. Your Teddy will be fine as long as you don't groom all the natural grease out of his coat" Beth said.

"Are you ready? Are you really ready?" her face was alight. "TADAA!!!"

Pushing ahead of me, she swung open the door and threw her arms wide open, encompassing the equivalent of the

Horse person's Holy Grail.

Beth's mum, Helen Wilcox, had been an eventer... pretty good... long-listed for the British team and all that stuff. One day she accidentally knocked over Charles (dad) who was considering suing her when he became mesmerised by her intelligent sparkling brown eyes and married her instead. Eventing as a career was rather forgotten as a quick succession of babies followed. Angie was first, then Tom. When she found them a really super lead rein pony called Bubbles (Shetland crossed with Welsh Mountain pony) it seemed a shame not to have more children to enjoy what a really good bombproof pony could offer. So followed Trixie, Maggie and then, after a break, Leo and finally Beth came along as a surprise to everyone. Rather sadly, Bubbles had gone to the Great Horse Playground in the sky by this time.

Charles came from a distinguished family of huntsmen and Masters of Hounds. He didn't much care for the chase, but enjoyed the prestige of belonging to a historical, respected family – and based his feed supplies business on the kudos surrounding the family name. Surprisingly down to earth, he rejected all the pomp and customs of his family, and set about creating his own empire in which his children could participate if they wished.

From a humble company selling oats, bran and subsequently pony nuts and coarse-mix, Charles, with his eldest son Tom in tow, created a huge company at the forefront of the revolution which saw basic feedstuffs being toned and tuned to supply a basic compound for every and any variation of horse. He saw where the market was heading and jumped in – not as a producer but a supplier.

The pet shop in town where I had first met Maggie reflected how this trend was also affecting dog and cat foods. It served as a pet shop, and also as a base for the horse feeds.

Lack of space eventually persuaded Charles and Tom to build a big ugly corrugated iron, box-profile structure to house the vast and colourful range of different horse feeds, as well as more recently converting a stone barn into the saddlery.

Meanwhile, Helen, after providing her many offspring with a pony each, was left with a stable full of lovely but outgrown little ponies. In a few small steps, she found herself teaching riding to endless small girls with pony-tails and dental braces, and Oak Tree Riding School was born. In those days, the industry was self-governing; no qualifications, no licences and no insurance required. She did eventually train as a riding instructor, and her first-born, Angie, dutifully followed her lead and became a qualified instructor too.

The second daughter, Trixie, told them where to stuff horses, wheelbarrows, wellies, mud and chilblains, and went off to business school.

Fortunately, she missed all the things she had spurned, and eventually did the prodigal thing and returned to the fold as business manager and accountant.

Maggie, aided by Aunty Carol who lived in town, became manager of the pet shop, whilst also supervising the livery yard and helping out in the super-duper new tack shop. Unlike the industrial-sized feed store, the saddlery was sited in a stone built, rustic barn of modest proportions. Classy, beautiful, and looking as if it was going to be very success-ful, every member of the family became dewy eyed when talking about it.

The last two children, Leo – blond, shaggy hair, tanned – looked more like a surfer or beach bum than the successful junior showjumper he'd become; his shock of fair hair was a babe magnet. Follow a string of gawping girls and you'll find Leo, Beth said. With pride.

Officially, Leo was in sixth form, but frequent letters from his school complained of too many absences and imminent A-level meltdown.

Beth, on the other hand, competed for fun and in a variety of disciplines. Yes, she did show-jumping but she also did Trec, hunter trials, eventing and even a bit of showing if she was in the mood. Winning wasn't the point; she was there to enjoy herself and give her beloved Zebedee an outing.

Note to self: Never ever never pass an opinion on ANYTHING related to horses in front of anyone in the Southward family. They have been involved in horses since the first tiny hippo… whatever… was the size of a dog living in a swamp in primordial soup… they probably know EVERYTHING there is to know.

p.s. do not reveal that you ride bareback, using pink balertwine as reins.

p.p.s. and don't tell them that you fell off TWICE

I'd never been in a tack shop before, and was amazed to feel excited by the sumptuousness… the richness of polished leather, shining stirrups, gleaming bits, all this overlaid by the strong smell of new leather.

For a moment I was reminded of the magnificence of an orchestra my ex-father had once taken me to see – the shining swatch of instruments in brass and silver and all the musicians wore formal black and white in sharp contrast to the brilliance of their instruments. I had been too young to appreciate the music and quickly grew bored, though I remember being fascinated by the percussionists dashing frantically back and forth among their range of toys.

How could there be so many things for horses? A horse lives in a field, eats grass, needs water and shelter… right?

Bbeeeeeppppp!   WRONG!

It seems a horse needs a stable with mangers, hay nets,

toys to dispel boredom, water buckets, feed buckets…

Rugs? What rugs? A horse grows a thick coat in winter so he's kept warm… in summer he sheds it… right?

Bbbbeeeep!   WRONG !

Well – not altogether wrong… but it seems some horses are clipped, shorn, denuded. And need… **TA-DAA**! to have their natural, hairy, greasy coats replaced by RUGS. (Excuse the following twelve page dissertation… to an ignorant non-horse person, this was a blinder).

Ideally, a turn-out rug should be waterproof, breathable and rip-stop(!). It can be heavyweight, lightweight and (you guessed it) medium weight. It may have shoulder gussets, leg straps, cross-surcingles, a fillet string, and be with or without a neck cover which ensures Dobbin is covered right to his ears.

Wait… not finished yet… Stable rugs similarly, different weights and often referred to as quilts! (get that!) I particularly liked the range of fleeces in wonderful jazzy colours, and so soft I wanted to wear one myself. I didn't dare say it out loud, but it was wasted on a horse who, in no less than five minutes would be bound to lie in dung, wee on it, cover it in straw or shavings and then chew it. I forgot to mention, fleeces come with matching leg and tail thingies, so petite pony is literally transformed into a brightly coloured, soft, cuddlesome thing you just want to sleep on.

In addition, there are summer sheets, coolers, anti-sweat rugs, day rugs, exercise sheets, shoulder guards, Lycra hoods (Oh purleez!) and total cover-all overalls to stop sweet-itch (whatever that is).

Forgive the tedium of this inventory, but it's a form of research for my next book 'What every parent should know before buying spoilt daughter a pony' This will, I know, all come as a shock.

I thought… pony… and rider, what d'you need? saddle, bridle, protective hat… right?

Bbbbeeeeeeeeppppppp! WRONG!

Saddles: showing, jumping, general purpose, show hunter, western, dressage, treeless or sheltie pad… and will that be english leather, synthetic or cheap and nasty imported stuff that any respectable saddler won't touch anyway. And don't forget, your new saddle comes naked… you also have to buy a girth, standard, elasticated, atherstone, balding, padded… etc and stirrups and the leathers that attach stirrups to saddle.

Even I'm bored with this now. It goes on and on. The saddle can be narrow, medium, wide, extra-wide, or so incredibly wide it would fit a table-top.

Here is the important bit: **it MUST fit the pony. And you.** You can't just bung any old saddle on a horse or you will give him a bad back, hurt him and, chances are, he'll be in so much pain he'll buck you off and never allow you near him again. So there!

Now I'm coming to the really good bit. Mesmerised by all this stuff that I'd never even dreamed of, I realised that I should really wear a hat… especially riding bareback and bridleless… I hear your hollow laughter! Jodhpurs would be good, too. Even in my brief journey into the world of haute ecole, and undignified descent from it - TWICE, I'd realised jeans rub, wrinkle up your leg and have a zip which sits exactly where you don't want it. You probably already know the range of materials, styles, colours and sizes jodhpurs come in, and they aren't bats wing style any more. In the family album is a photo of my gran wearing these weird baggy batwings. Modern fabrics actually reveal every blob of cellulite and visible panty line and anything else you might not want the world to see!

Beth had abandoned me in favour of changing Zeb's damp rug after pointing out the racks of jods, jackets, waterproofs and shelves of hats, boots, gloves, wellies, muckers, socks... you name it... it was there.

When Beth disappeared, leaving me to browse, I darted back to the rows of jods and went pale when I saw the prices. There were some that were cheaper than the smart canary-yellow showing ones; every colour and combination of colours imaginable faced me... and in cotton/spandex, polyester/cotton, lycra, multi-stretch, two-tone, three-tone, ribbed, elastane... you get the idea?

Personally, I needed something dark and workmanlike; it hadn't escaped my attention that Teddy seemed to cover me in a silvery grease every time I went near him – not to mention the slobber! Then, of course, there was the small matter of spending much of my riding time under the hedge or in puddles! Imagine my delight when I found a big basket marked 'shop soiled' full of jods in all shapes and sizes.

Of course, I was sneakily rooting through them hoping to find my size in a sensible navy or black when Beth caught me. I hate blushing. How can one ever be cool when one's face flames like a cooked sausage all the time? I've noticed that Beth can be quite tactful, and looks the other way but this time she barged in with "Oh, d'you need jods? you should have said... Angie will find you a pair... there are loads in the back... ANGIE!"

Ah! so the manager of the day was Angie! I'd wondered, which sister it was... I seemed to have been introduced to so many of them, I was totally confused! Next thing I was ushered into a changing room with a selection of jods and found myself staring at Me as Horsewoman. Yeah, yeah, yeah... they do show everything and I had the feeling I would wear a big baggy jumper over them. Crazy when you recall that I've spent most of my life in a leotard, which is not a kind garment!

When I'd chosen a pair of needlecord navy jods, Beth and Angie and I had a big argument about money. They wanted me to have them free as they were, I was assured, destined for the bin. In the end, they accepted £5.

Okay – I knew they were humouring me but at least I didn't feel like a bludger who'd only gone there to get stuff on the cheap.

"Now…" Beth began "what about a hat? You really do need one, you know…"

"Not until I'm riding him…" I evaded the subject.

"So the jods were just to pose in?" sneaky.

"Erm… well… I'm mainly doing sort-of… er… leading him… you know, taking him for walks… and things…" I finished lamely. It wasn't altogether untruthful.

"Let's go and have a cup of tea…" Beth's voice was firm. She led the way to the huge family kitchen and sat me down at the big scrubbed table. All the other 900 family members seemed to have vanished.

"… I don't want to interfere…" Beth began hesitantly (don't you hate it when somebody does that; you know they're going to put the hard-sell on you…).

"Sugar?"

I nodded, and added "Two please" an indulgence denied during my days as a gymnast.

She plonked two mugs on the table, slopping slightly, then brought a packet of custard creams, ripped open the packaging and offered me one.

"Sara… if you, like, need any help with… um… your pony… or with riding…" she nibbled the corner of her biscuit "you will ask, won't you…"

Beth was very pretty with small pointy features and

fantastic cheek-bones. Her hair formed a dark cloud round her face, not curly and not frizzy, but somewhere in-between. I wondered how her brother was so very blond when the other children were so dark.

"Thanks…" I said, then added in a rush "Yes… I will ask when I need help. At the moment I just want to explore the whole horse thing with an open mind." I paused and then said "and I need time to build a relationship with Teddy. He's been on his own for ages with no-one caring for him and I need him to trust me"

"It's just that… well…" Beth was searching for a diplomatic way through this "you know… horses are big and strong… and can really take the mick when they think they can get away with it… It's a bit like dealing with children. You have to be firm and kind and patient…"

"He's a sweetie" I said, feeling a rush of love for him.

"Yeah… but half a tonne of horse can be a…" she giggled "handful!"

"Thanks" I said, realising this was difficult for her. We'd come a long way from the grunts of the other day.

"I'm not that great…" Beth said "… but if you want riding lessons… I could maybe help"

"Not great!" I spluttered. "You won a red rosette!"

At first I thought she was choking on a biscuit crumb, she laughed and coughed so much. Eventually, she sipped her tea, swallowed and cleared her throat and said "It was a rosette. It isn't that difficult to win one"

"Isn't it?" I asked, surprised "I thought it would be"

"Yes. It is. No. it isn't… I have a fantastic pony… he's the winner"

"You're just being modest." I protested.

"Zeb and I… we have a good relationship. But he's the brilliant one, not me. He could win with any other rider because he's so talented. I couldn't win with any other pony" Beth explained.

I felt a bit of a dork because I really didn't know whether this was true or not.

"When you get going" Beth promised "I'll let you ride him. And" she shouted "I'll let you compete him… then you'll see…"

"In your dreams!" I laughed, but liked the idea that I might be good enough to ride him one day.

I couldn't wait to get home to my pony… to try on my jods and maybe have another go at getting myself thrown off. All in the interests of experience, you understand.

"Before that, though…" Beth said "I shall lend you a hat. I've got loads… there must be one that will fit you. Then I won't worry about you falling off"

"Moi. Falling off?" I asked in hurt innocence.

But I had my fingers crossed behind my back.

Chapter 8

The next Sunday was like waiting for an execution… Mine. My mother tiptoed around me, knowing that I would rip off her face if she said the wrong thing. "Would you like to go out for tea?" she asked at one point "… my treat"

"No" I snarled, wishing she would go out for a few hours so that I could ride Teddy. Notice I say 'ride'. Such is my arrogance that I actually visualised myself as a proper rider. At least I had learned from the kids at Oak Tree that you don't dismount by swinging your leg forwards and kicking poor Dobbin in the head. I even had a rough idea how to mount, though how that could be achieved from a step-ladder and with no saddle, I was not sure. And the reason for standing with your back to the pony's head and probably getting a hefty bite on your back-side was still ambiguous in my head.

My mother wouldn't go out because she was waiting for somebody. She said this in such a way that I envisaged a welcome visitor and a nice surprise. Er? It turned out to be Jim the Skim's 'lad'. Why? What?

My crafty parent had seen the possibility of some cheap labour. The 'lad' turned out to be called Wayne, Shane or Duane. Not sure which… although now proudly a 'working man' he had only in the past year renounced Grunting in favour of Normal Speech, and it was taking a lot of effort to enunciate words clearly after spending so long as a Neanderthal.

WSD was delighted to be offered the chance of some extra money through a back-pocket job which was, of course, to be kept secret from the Worthy Plasterer. It also gave him a chance to be top dog for a while, and discuss tasks 'like a man' with much rubbing at his currently beardless chin. Mum flirted a little and the poor lad blushed so violently that he made my pink moments look like peaches and cream. Bless!

WSD was given the task of sizing the walls where the plaster had dried. Like… YES!!!… my bedroom and my study. Plastered walls, apparently, soak up emulsion paint so fast that the brush nearly vanishes into the wall. No such thing as 'working' the paint. It goes spluuullllssss and is gone. Sizing is simply the process of sealing the plaster with a gooey thin wallpaper paste (so ah-ha, he's called Wayne!) informed me in the tone of a grown-up speaking to a thick toddler. Don't care; he can get off on being patronising if he wants to… he's sizing MY walls. That's all that matters!

Mother settled Wayne down with all the ceilings and walls in my TWO! rooms to size… and if he finished that, he could start on her bedroom, methinks this poor sucker is going to have to come and live in, she has such elaborate plans for his spare time. Duane… Wayne… needs the money as he is, he informed me in reverent tones, saving up for a motorbike. I guess it's going to be an all noise and no speed job; you know, nought to thirty in ten minutes; and its engine will be all revved out within six months but little lad'll be happy!

Under my breath I was muttering incantations to my mother: please go to **B&Q**… I really wanted to er… sit on

Teddy again and her presence was not wanted. When she started tidying up in the midget caravan I casually asked "not going to **B&Q** today?"

"No. I need to go to Sainsburys later..." No. Go Now.

"I've had an idea for my bedroom..." I began and saw her expression brighten. Anything that hinted I was settling in was better than Serious Grunting. Girl-talk about paint colours was something she could handle. Her expression was mother giving serious consideration to daughter's daft ideas.

"Indian" I said, trying to calm the rage her face ignited in me.

"Indian?"

"You know... really rich fabrics, with glittery mirrors... every shade from pink to scarlet..."

I wasn't sure that her enthusiasm was genuine, but she tried. "Oh yeah! I was in a shop in town last week... and it was full of these gorgeous fabrics and cushions... very eastern... so sumptuous I wanted to roll in them"

Sounded genuine. "So..." I began but she interrupted "I even picked up a catalogue..." and cantered out to her car where I could hear her huffing and puffing as she rooted about in the boot. Red faced, she reappeared, waving it. Yes, it was gorgeous. Just what I had in mind.

"So..." I started "if I'm using a bedspread something like... er... that" I stubbed my finger down on a picture "with rich curtains and cushions and stuff... d'you think I should go for white walls?... otherwise it's going to be a bit, er, much... What d'you think?"

Sometimes, I'm so phoney, I hate myself. I already knew exactly what I would choose, but wanted her to think she was having an input.

Head on one side, flicking pages "Well... white's a bit

stark... what about a really rich clotted cream?"

Clotted cream. I sniggered and changed it into a bit of throat clearing. She pointed to a picture in the book "look... like that... d'you think that works?"

"Lovely" I smiled at her, my eyes a little glazed. Just Go.

"I could go to **B&Q** and bring some... if you want..." tentatively.

"Would you... that would be great... maybe I could start it during the evenings..." I said, then adding bitterly "unless I'm bogged down by homework..."

"Okay... I'll go and get some and do the shopping as well" she said crisply, closing the subject.

Earlier, she had said "Sahara... I know you must be worried about starting a new school tomorrow. I want you to understand that you WILL go to school. If you feel sick, if your period starts, if you fall and break your neck... you will go to school." Eyeing me beadily, she said "So don't waste energy trying to think up some excuse for not going. Do you understand me?"

"Moi?!" I asked, and laughed, knowing this would disarm her.

Sometimes I really hate her; she can be too damn clever.

"Right..." she was tossing cushions aside, looking for her car keys as usual. Just Go! In the interests of hastening her departure, I helped her to look. Of course, she had just been outside to fetch the catalogue from her car. The keys were dangling from the lock of the boot.

"I'll make Shane Wayne a cup of tea" I told her. "You have a nice time..." chivvying her towards the pigmy steps out of the caravan.

"Shopping?" she asked sarcastically.

"No... in **B&Q**..." I smiled.

After the car had driven out of sight, I flew up the stairs

in the house two at a time and breathlessly asked Duane Shane "Can you wait a while for a brew?" noticing that the slimy size he was using had been flung onto ceiling, windows and floor, as well as the walls. Oh well… maybe they needed sealing too…

Teddy screaming across the field at a flat out gallop, erased all negative thoughts from my head. For now… for this moment… I could forget the horror of an impending new school, could shift from the constant sense of loss I felt, my ex-father, friends, old school, gymnastics… even the old me! and enjoy this great uncomplicated relationship with a horse.

Tufty lumps of dead hair had gradually been eased away from the lower line of his stomach; it had taken a lot of work, but he was looking better. I had smothered his mane and tail in baby oil and worked with my fingers, easing out the knots and tangles. One day I would have the nerve to trim his tail, but for the moment could just about live with it trailing in the mud. His lovely chocolate brown coat was even starting to develop a hint of sheen. I congratulated myself, he definitely looks a lot better now!

Smart (yeah!) in my new navy jodhpurs, I resisted the impulse to clamber on board straight away, but first did some leading about and trying to teach him to respond to particular words. With no bridle, I was dependent on his good nature. On the ground, he was great. He stopped when I stopped, walked when I walked, turned and circled and moved sideways at the touch of my hand on his belly. On the ground, though, was a bit different from being perched up there where he couldn't see much of me.

Fearing the Return of The Mummy, though, I couldn't spend too much time leading him – not if I was to hone my falling skills. Stepladder. Pony. Okay… so far so good. The ladder didn't bother him, even when it wobbled as I leaned forward to swing my leg over his back. Breathe, breathe, I instructed myself, wrapping my fingers into his thick black mane.

Aha! C'mon!

C'MON!!!!

With a bit of wriggling, I centred myself on his back, breathed deeply, let everything hang loose............ waited............... breathed............... When his head dropped lower, I gave a gentle bump with both legs and

WEYHEY! my wonderful pony walked forward smoothly.

Only one small burp in the full belly of life... Shane Wayne Duane's pale spotty face was pressed to the window in my bedroom. Watching.

One more reason not to make a total fool of myself by falling off, then.

Should I happen to break my neck, crack my head or fracture several of my appendages, at least he'll be able to summon the paramedics.

Love the smell of horse.

Love the feel of horse moving beneath me.

Love the wind gently lifting my pony's mane.

Love the sweetness of him; unconditional, non-judgemental forgiving...

We were getting better at this stuff, my pony and I. With less slithering around, I seemed to have found where my weight should be in relation to his centre of gravity. As a gymnast, these are matters of great importance.

My hips seemed to be in synch with his movement, and I could feel each hind leg stepping forward underneath his body with a lovely swinging motion.

If I let my legs hang really long down his sides, we were both more comfortable. As soon as I tried, say, gripping with my knees, my bottom seemed to come up off his back and that made me tilt forward. I somehow felt as though my two seat-bones were where they needed to be so that I wouldn't interfere with his movement.

Lots of halts and walking on again established communication. Even with only the flimsy pink twine for reins, Teddy was responding to me. Very, very satisfying!

Straight lines, circles, stops, starts. More straight lines, circle the other way, stops, starts. What my body did was persuading him to respond; it felt smooth and easy.

Yeah! Well… It did until I sort of nudged a bit more with my legs and… well… off he went!

Hanging onto mane and 'reins' saved me from an ignoble dismount.

What I have learned today: trotting is very bouncy.

But wait. The other thing I have learned today is that cantering is GREAT!

Cantering, I hear you gasp with horror! It was an accident. The trot was chucking me about so much that I did something (don't know what) and we were… well… floating… dreaming… ecstatic…

Aware that Teddy had spent the past year standing in a field, short of food, I knew he wasn't fit. Too much cantering could harm him. But… one small problem… how to stop?

Keeping him on a circle meant that his speed was fairly consistent and controlled, but if I hollered 'Whoa!' he would probably slow down to trot. From canter, the trot would be fast and choppy… my bottom was NOT glued to him… I wasn't sure that it would stay anywhere near him. Visions of another undignified exit loomed large.

Grabbing hanks of mane in both hands, I breathed down into my legs and feet, prepared for a parachute(less) landing, made a short prayer that he wouldn't over-react and skid to a halt with his nose buried in the ground, and said gently in a very low voice "wwwwhhhhoooooaaaa".

For a moment we continued our rocking-horse canter round the circle. I disentangled my hands enough to pull on the pink twine, breathed down, down and repeated "wwwwhhhhooooaaa". What a star! What a treasure! My fantastic pony slowed down to a trot, this time a smooth rounded pace that I somehow managed to sit through as I repeated stages 1 and 2 and he slowed down to walk.

My cup runneth over! Coaxing him to a halt, I heard my mother's car on the lane, remembered that Wayne had never been watered and may well have expired with dehydration. Too late. I had time only to dismount – elegantly now I knew which way to swing myself – take the headcollar off my warm damp pony and make a run for the wheelbarrow... as though all the time I'd been shovelling his droppings out of the field.

"Got your paint" Mum remarked cheerily as she passed the field gate. "Fancy a brew?"

"Er... yes... I guess Shane Wayne will be ready for one now as well..." I was still rather breathless, but hoped the Airhead parent might put that down to me shovelling shit, It was only as I emptied the barrow that I realised she may have, actually, being a parent she WOULD have, noticed the jodhpurs!

That afternoon – the final day of my freedom as a dispossessed person of No Fixed Educational Establishment – two things happened.

Beth arrived in a clop of clicking footfalls on a pony who wasn't Zebedee.

Teeth gnashing, I noted the beaming parent's expression... huge delight that I had a 'little' friend and was therefore settling in to the country life; also it was good for the rural image to have people on horses arriving on one's doorstep.

"I'm not staying" Beth said. "This is a new pony who

hasn't seen much traffic so I offered to hack over here and let him see the sights. What a pity you aren't riding Teddy yet… we could have gone for a hack together"

"Mmmmmm"

"Oh" I'd never seen Beth so talkative "and I brought you… " thrusting the reins into my hands, she tugged the rucksack off her back and unbuckled it "Ta-daa… a hat… try it on…"

"How very kind" my smug mother simpered "I'm sure this will encourage Sara to start riding…" but there was a gleam in her eye that I didn't like.

"Try it on" Beth ordered "then if it isn't right I can bring you a different one when we pick you up for school tomorrow" Aaaaaargh! She used the S word. I hissed at her and made the sign of the cross with my two index fingers.

"Sara!" my mother scolded, plonking the hat on my head. It felt alright, but Beth tilted it this way and that, checking that it would stay on if I should have a fall (as if) "It has to be right." she told me. "Nearly right isn't good enough… and…" she rapped her knuckles on the top of it "… you wear it EVERY time you ride…"

"Yes ma'am" I said meekly.

"Seriously…" she gave the chin strap one last tweak "if you ride, you will fall… it isn't just something that happens to other people. A friend of mine was seriously brain-damaged in a very small fall on grass because she wasn't wearing a hat" I nodded my head in what I hoped was a serious way.

Wayne came past, wheeling his push-bike, smiled and blushed at Mum, noticed me in the riding hat and said "Oh good, only an idiot rides one of those dangerous beasties without a hat"

Die, insect!

***

Deep in the unexplored caverns of my subconscious, something was stirring. It seemed the idea of an exotic Eastern boudoir had nudged some alien sleeping thing into life. Craving... I was craving for some un-named glamorous sensual luxury.

All my aware life had been spent training in Gymnastics. I've no idea what a hair shirt is, but I imagine it's a garment that almost drives you mad with itchiness... and worn, in some way, to subdue the spirit or the flesh... or whatever it was those sick old Church guys felt should be overcome. Now I was no longer addicted to the screaming endorphins of endless physical activity, I realised how stark and austere my life had been. I trained; I did necessary school stuff; I trained; I slept. My diet was totally governed by rules of nutrition; my trainer checked me, poked, prodded, weighed, assessed and told me in the most minute detail what I could and couldn't eat. Long-suffering female parent went along with it – without any thanks or appreciation – because I insisted on sticking to it 24/7.

Bed was somewhere to sleep... to rest tired bones. It was not a place for frivolity. My pastel coloured room in the old house was as featureless and without character as a nun's cell.

My hair was shorn and therefore easy to shower – several times a day depending on training schedules. I poked at my muscles and searched for any signs of blubber or weakness. My body was hard; my life was hard. When my ex's mother, never to be known as Gran because it 'aged her so', said "Darling... I know your floor routine is very graceful... .but isn't it... well..." searching for words 'not very feminine' then backed off when she read DEATH in my expression. Ridiculous woman, I thought.

Sensual was not a word I understood.

Very sadly... FUN was also not a word I understood.

Teddy had given me more thrills and smiles than I'd experienced in years. My hair was growing longer. Hard muscles had softened slightly already, despite an exercise programme so rigorously adhered to that it was as much a part of my day as brushing my teeth. Feeling different... I was... I dunno... letting go... relaxing. I loved the idea of having a bedroom full of gorgeous fabrics and colours, and smells... maybe incense... oh yes! and as yet, hard to imagine... me – lounging around. Not in the mindless switched-off way I'd done when I was first dragged kicking and screaming to this end of the world building site.

***

I would have walked Teddy up the lane to keep Beth company, but he was so agitated at the sight of the little grey Nipper, I wasn't sure I could handle him in just a headcollar.

"Shall I bring you a bridle next time I come?" Beth asked.

My mother, overhearing said "No need... I'm sure I saw a bridle and a saddle in the tack room." Now she tells me! "We needed somewhere to store rubbish, so pushed it all into every space we could find. Maybe it's time we had a clear out" looking meaningfully at me.

"Okay, I'll do it tomorrow" I snapped.

"Nice try, but you won't be here tomorrow" smiling sweetly at me.

"I could come over next weekend and give you a hand?" Beth suggested.

"That would be fantastic" my mother raved. Ask me, why don't you!

I grunted and wished my mother would go and play with something noxious in the potting shed.

"I'd better get going" Beth picked up the vibes "and take this little animal back to his stable." Fastening her chin strap, she checked the girth, put her foot in the stirrup and swung herself effortlessly onto the pony's back. Hmmm… Glad I didn't offer her the use of my step-ladder!

"See you in the morning…"

"SSSSSSSSS. Wash out your filthy mouth!" I shouted at her and heard her laughter above the clopping of hooves as she trotted up the lane.

Warm weather; we scavenged through various outbuildings for anything suitable for sitting outside. A beautiful picnic table and comfortable chairs would have been great, but hey! who wants luxury? We dusted off a couple of white moulded plastic picnic chairs and also found a few folding canvas chairs which looked slightly dodgy where frame met fabric. In an emergency, maybe we would use them.

Normally I shunned my mother's company, but something about the scent- laden afternoon, and a certain satisfaction with my progress in the Equitation Department, had mellowed me. Mum was wearing a billowing floaty skirt with tiny purple sprigged flowers embroidered on it (Charity Shop, honest! She had sworn when I first admired it). Hair loose and swinging silkily around her shoulders, she was my hippie beatnik flower power mamma. So I graciously accepted the offer of a mug of tea and a chunk of carrot-cake. A new experience for me! NOT allowed when I was in training!

Sitting on the white plastic chair, she swung her bare feet up onto one of the unused chairs and gave a little mew of pleasure. "Isn't this just paradise…?" she murmured. "It's so quiet… you can hardly hear any traffic… just birds and trees and the breeze"

I grunted non-committally and she shaded her eyes with one hand to look at me. If she starts asking whether I'm happy here or not, I will trap her fingers in a folding chair and head for the hills. She's learning; she said no more.

"Did you see Teddy when Beth came down the lane on Nipper?" I changed the subject.

"Poor lamb" she said licking butter cream off a finger "He's so lonely. It must have been awful for him all this time... like keeping a prisoner in solitary confinement. Even worse for a horse because they're herd animals... they should never be kept on their own"

"I hadn't thought of that" I've already told you, I know nothing about horses. "What can we do about it?"

"Don't even GO there!" She warned.

"Where? What?" I asked indignantly.

"Getting a companion for him" she smiled.

"Your thoughts, not mine" I said grimly. "I'd never even realised he was lonely until I saw him doing an impression of an Arab stallion along the hedge."

"You can't really use a word like 'magnificent' about a chunky pony like Teddy" she said "but in his own way he was quite spectacular, wasn't he?" and we both laughed fondly.

After, I said "Is he really lonely?"

"Yes. Definitely. Look at the way he seeks our company." Mum swiped her thumb round her plate, taking up the last crumbs. I still feel so guilty about 'indulgences' that I have to leave a few morsels! "He bonded with you so quickly because he needs a herd"

"So it wasn't me as a horse-magnet? Not my attractive personality? Not that he recognised me as a soul-mate?" Omygod! I'm having a conversation with my mother!

"Obviously!" she stressed the word "all those things... but loneliness as well"

"So what can we do about it?" an image of selling him to a family who kept other horses caught my heart in a tight grip. Quickly I added "He can stay here, can't he?" Did my voice sound pleading then? I hope not.

"I hope so." her eyes were reading my face "I think he's important in our lives at the moment... long term, I'm not sure we can afford him." turning away from me.

Not ready to beg; not ready for you to know what I feel, how I feel. Can't do this now... I feel like I'm on the edge of a precipice. I drained my mug and plonked it down on the wobbly table that formed the centrepiece of our designer (not) picnic set.

Mum's head shot up "Was that a car?" We live near the bottom of the lane, so there is almost no passing traffic. Occasionally the farmer passes on his way to the field that has an access just beyond our land. It's amusing how quickly we've defined our boundaries and man our barricades. We both listened. There was a gentle clunk which only the doors on expensive cars make when closing.

A car with an engine that is almost inaudible; a car with leather upholstery and a waft of perfume... and... stricken, my mother and I eyed each other.

"Lilian" she mouthed as a voice called "Coooo-eeee darlings, here we are!" and my grandmother breezed round the corner of the house.

"Oh" said mother.

"Oh" said I.

"Surprise, surprise... " chirped the woman who spawned my son-of-Satan ex-father.

"How did you find us?" my mother's voice was faint.

"Dahlings!" she brushed the air near my mother's cheek with a parody of a kiss. Wanting to avoid such close contact, I leapt to my feet shouting "Where's Gramps? Is he with you?" as my beleaguered grandfather appeared round the corner of the house, carrying several carrier bags, a rug, and a cake-box.

Taking some of the bags from him, I kissed his cheek and asked "How are you? I've missed you".

"What a mess this whole business is" he sighed "I'm so sorry for what he's done"

"It must be hard for you, too"

"Yes, but I've always known he was a pillock"

I snorted with glee, and received a reproving glare from Lilian, real name Lily, but she changed it when a girl in her class called her Lil. So common! Personally, I'd have thought that a longer name was more likely to be abbreviated, but hey! what do I know about nobs! Actually, she isn't… just aspires to be one!

"So…" her beady eye travelled around the dusty, rubbish tip of a lawn, to the unkempt hedges, apart from the bit I'd pruned with help from Edward Scissorhands, rather scruffy assortment of sheds and stables and eventually came to rest on the rear of the house.

I must warn you, Lilian's role model has always been Lady Catherine de Burgh from *Pride and Prejudice*. She doesn't quite carry it off, being short of true blue blood, but amazingly, she actually admires her. Every new *P & P* film or BBC adaptation has to be watched so that she can, as it were, develop her character.

She has a weakness, this Grandmere of mine, and that is her son, my Ex. My mother's Ex. Once she forgot herself and called him Precious. Mum never allowed him to recover from that, but when she used it, it was in the voice of Gollum from Lord of the Rings, and included a lot of hissing. My Precioussssss…

Remembering how at first he had found it funny, and then increasingly irritating, I felt sad. Long ago, there had been good moments, and fun. Where does love go? Mum and Dad really did love each other once upon a time. Now they pale if the other is mentioned.

"Darling" my well-dressed, powdered, handbag-toting ancestor is saying " your father really does miss you" I was annoyed that she had taken advantage of Mum heading off into the tin-box to make tea, to start her manipulating.

"Tough" I answered rudely.

"Sahara!" her face was shocked. I may be a grump but I'm not usually rude.

"Oh, for goodness sake… He left us, you know. We did nothing wrong"

Hearing my raised voice, Mum's worried face appeared in the tiny doorway.

"There are two sides to every story" Lilian snapped.

Snubbing her, I turned my back and said to Gramps "Why didn't you ring? I could have looked forward to seeing you then"

"Sorry, chuck. It was your Gran's idea to surprise you" he smiled "I thought it was rather… er… inappropriate… in the circumstances"

"Too right!" my mother said, picking her way between piles of bricks and lengths of wood with a tray bearing four mugs of tea. Lilian hates mugs. Her little rosebud mouth can't quite cope with thick pot – she needs delicate china, what with being well bred and having a delicate constitution. (Not!)

I grinned at Mum, knowing she'd deliberately done it to annoy her mother-in-law. Lilian tutted, but managed not to verbalise her complaint.

Gramps smiled into his mug – knowing what we were all playing at. Bless him, he's such a lovely man and doesn't deserve to have wasted so much of his life on a skinny version of Hyacinth Bouquet. "Alright, mum?" my mother asked her innocently. I spluttered into my tea. Lilian glared at us all. "Is it any wonder?" she asked cryptically.

"D'you want to come and see the pony, Gramps?"

"A pony? You've got a pony?" Lilian squealed "How much did that cost? Is your father going to pay for its keep?"

An awkward silence stilled us all. Mum looked at me and pointed her head towards the field, giving me permission to go; Gramps scurried after me, looking relieved.

"Sara. I'm sorry…" he began as we leaned our elbows on the top of the gate and watched my gorgeous Teddy trotting towards us, nickering happily. "This whole business has slightly unhinged her."

"Yeah. Right!" I laughed. "She's always been like this."

"She doesn't mean half of it… she gets caught up in her own version of reality. And you know how much she dotes on… him" Gramps sighed. Teddy snuffled at our arms and hands, but everybody had warned me against giving titbits, so he searched in vain.

"What a corker!" Gramps said, scratching his neck. Does everybody in the world, except me, know how to relate to horses. Have they all had horses when they were young? Did they all have lessons?

"He's lovely. He was left here by the previous owners… I've been cleaning up his field… it was disgusting with years of poo piled everywhere… maybe the grass will grow soon… he's a bit thin really because he's been so neglected…"

"I'll pay for his keep" Gramps said.

"What?"

""You are – and always will be – my granddaughter. My idiot son may have tiptoed into pastures new; I'm not interested in a newer model" he said "You will get everything I ever intended to give you; that includes love and money. If you need help with this animal's keep, then I'll provide it."

"Gramps…"

"No... let me say this..." he paused "I have loved you since the moment you were put into my arms in the hospital where you were born. I want to know what you're doing. I want to be your granddad. I'm not trying to buy you... but I'll be damned if that pathetic specimen of a father of yours will take what's rightfully yours." His eyes were decidedly misty "I'll transfer a certain amount each month into your bank account... it's what you would have had eventually if that clown hadn't been guided by his pants instead of his brain..."

Teddy's head shot up as my mother appeared. "There you are. Lilian's ready to go" she called.

"Chop chop" Gramps mumbled "She wants to go, we gotta go..."

Lilian was thrusting the contents of the carrier bags onto the wobbly picnic table. My mother, standing behind her, was almost helpless with suppressed laughter.

"Beans... cheap and full of protein" Lilian was saying "Dried milk in case you run out of the proper stuff... tins of soup..."

"Good God!" Gramps shouted "It's not a war zone"

"No need to take that tone" Lilian sniffed "I'm doing my duty here"

As though suddenly possessed, I heard myself say "Love would be good. Duty sounds rather dry and musty, don't you think?"

"Pardon?" my grandmother pulled herself to full height and her eyes blazed at me.

"Duty, Granny... is rather loveless. That's all I was saying" I explained.

"Your manners could be improved, Sahara" she snapped.

"Right... I think it's time to go" Gramps tried to rescue the situation. Too late, daggers had been drawn.

"Your attitude, Sahara, is because you are so young. You may be angry at your daddy, but when you are older and more grown up, you will understand…"

Battle lines were drawn then. A red mist of rage filled my head.

My dotty grandmother had twisted reality so that she could forgive her precious son.

Frozen in the moment, I saw my mother's mouth form a perfect pink O. My grandfather's face was old and terrified. Lilian was pulling on her gloves, oblivious to the effect she'd created.

Very softly I said "Of course, Granny, you may be wrong… I do realise that when he abandoned me and Mum for a younger model he was thinking solely of himself. D'you know, Mum got to keep me and he got the dog?"

Lilian's mouth was opening and closing, but no fish-like bubbles wafted upwards. I said "and then he had the dog put down because it wasn't convenient. Good job I ended up with Mum, isn't it?"

Turning, I walked away in gymnast mode, my toes touching the ground gracefully, then the heels. Back straight. Tears pouring down my face.

10 THINGS I LOVE ABOUT MY HORSE

First: Humbly he stands grounded as I drench him with tears. Howling and sobbing, I clutch handfuls of his coarse black mane and smear snot on it. No tissues, no hugs, no counselling. Wrapping myself in the warmth of his being, I am allowed to purge myself. Does he wish that from deep cloistered caverns of memory, he too could release pain through sobbing?

Do horses weep silent tears?

Second: When it's over, without fuss, without advice or platitudes, without long confused goodbyes, he wanders away and eats grass.

Third: While I stress about new school, colour of carpet for my bedroom, and stew over a traitorous grandmother, Teddy greets friends with joy, farts unashamedly and dreams in the sun.

Fourth: Travelling the wilderness, the herd moves on before it sours the land. Horses don't burn holes in the ozone layer, pollute rivers and oceans, contaminate the soil, waste resources or squander the future. Best of all – they don't eat humans!

Fifth: As a non-horse person, I've seen green fields full of multi-coloured horses and never given them a second thought. They're just animals, aren't they? Stuff food in one end, it comes out the other and they're a convenient shape for sitting on.

Way back in history, some ancient guy with food stains on his clothes pronounced 'Animals have no souls', and that made it okay for us to hunt, trap, slaughter, eat, abuse, or neglect whatever living creatures we chose to

Standing in the sun with my pony, tears drying on my cheeks, I watch his ears flickering back and forth, attentive, latching onto me, registering sounds in stereo. That long horse face is so expressive. Eyes, soft and gentle can, in fear, roll wild and white. Relaxed muzzle tightens in stress, becoming wrinkled and hard.

Don't tell me this pony feels nothing.

Sixth: Feel how big a horse is – big in spirit. His love, or whatever that may be in horse terms, is unconditional and forgiving. Patiently he struggles to interpret our garbled messages and turn them into instructions he can fulfil.

The effort is all on his side.

The English abroad have no patience with 'foreigners' speaking their native language. How many horse-people actually try to speak Horse?

Seventh: Nameless, wild, untamed, primordial horse, dog-like and tiny, scented the wind blowing dust across the explosive primeval planet. Rooted deep in his genes, an ancient fear of huge flying creatures shaped his primitive instincts.

To allow people on his back is a monumental act of trust.

Eighth: He is very gentle. His humour is kind. He is not embarrassed to smear me with green slobber.

Ninth: Beneath his appearance, whatever that may be, from Shetland to War-horse lies a huge spirit, so forgiving and so pure that it wouldn't stoop to playing mind-games and yet has a mischievous sense of fun.

Tenth: Not pushy, not judgemental, not critical. His attitude says gimme grass and you can be whatever you want.

Chapter 9

You want school stories? Go and read 'Third form at Mallory Towers'. Immerse yourself in Sweet Valley High.

School is school is school. Get through each day, come home and live.

Ask me what I want to do when I 'grow up'. Duh!

That's the problem... until I burn with passion about some career, how can I care whether I get good grades?

New school.

Help me! I wanna get off.

Let me out!

My Inner Monster, who, has been pathetically quiet lately, doesn't know how to deal with so many new faces, new names. Growling doesn't seem quite the way to go.

Maggie picked me up; I was in my shiny new uniform; would have loved to roll in mud or let Teddy do his worst with hairs, runny nose and green saliva but I knew how dearly all this new gear had cost my mum. I mean, she could have bought a dozen tins of really good varnish with the money... or a new door-knocker. Chattering happily in an attempt, no doubt, to take my mind off the ordeal to come, Maggie simply pushed Beth and I into grunting mode again. We were almost at school when Beth told her to 'shut it!' and she did.

Mentor, Minder and Monitor, Beth nudged me in the right direction all day. She wasn't heavy or over-indulgent, and most of the time ignored me. When I needed to find my way somewhere important – like toilet and canteen – she was there. So I didn't get lost or wet my pants or die of dehydration. When she introduced me to her friends it was like "Sara... Lucy" and left us to talk or not.

Mainly not.

Social skills aren't exactly my thing: I've spent too much time on the beam and high bars to have learned how to do small talk.

Roughly, this is how it goes.

Girls: want a new Best Friend. At this age, desperate to be loved, anything will do – male or female or - hate to say it - Horse.

Safely incarcerated in a picture, it will often be a Pop Singer. Girls wear this person like a badge of honour... his name scrawled on pencil-case, a picture of him glued to school-bag, a teen-mag give-away picture of him on a badge.

One at a time, they sidle up and coyly introduce themselves. This is the equivalent of dogs sniffing each other's bottoms and parading around in a bizarre stiff-legged way.

It goes something like this 'Phew... I'm Amy. English next... are you okay... settling in alright? if you, er, like need to know about anything... just like, er, ask...' and at this point will subtly wave pencil-case or badge to establish which camp she's in. This is where it all goes wrong because, according to the script, I'm supposed to get excited and say 'Oh... I love Tom from McFly... or Robbie... or Duncan or even Beyonce!'

But... I start stammering and say "Oh thanks... I'll remember that..." Off she goes, deflated that I'm not The One.

Cue Carol wafting a hand on which she's written HARRY in biro... and same scenario.

One by one I disappoint them all.

Except Beth and her friends who are more likely to have pictures of ponies stuck on their exercise books. If I really want to please them, I'll have to stick Teddy's photo on my calculator. Then again, maybe not.

So it goes on. Occasionally there's a spark and a hint that a real conversation could start. All the other girls standing in pretty little clumps within earshot, prick up their little pink ears and want to be catty. Not bitchy... that comes later when I have definitely been rejected as a possible friend; at the moment I'm a maybe.

How did I get to be so oafish and ungracious, I hear you thinking. I guess it's just the way I am. When I was training, I hadn't time for all that stuff. Addicted, I worked, trained; any socialising was with people who spoke the language... who would understand why I almost died with excitement after managing a 'full twisting double back, double pike... Arabian... triple spin' or whatever...

Now – I've almost forgotten the language. And have nothing to replace it with.

Boys: on the other hand, hunt in packs.

My theory is that some physiological defect prevents adolescent boys raising their eyes above boob level.

I have some sympathy with the elaborate Grunt language they've developed due to the unpredictable nature of breaking voices; one minute they sing soprano, the next they squawk like a flattened barnyard fowl.

Gathered in groups, the young un-Braves' eyes sidle to boobs, bum, legs. In that order. That's it. At this age they aren't aware that girls also have eyes, faces and brains.

Studying their scuffed shoes, they grunt and nudge each

other, then exchange foxy sidelong glances. It's noticeable that without exception, their school collar and tie are always far too wide for their scrawny necks. Spotty skin also desperately needs concealer.

Living a life apart from the weedy, pasty-faced, spotty, unintelligible herd are

TA-DAAAAA!!!!

The Footie Lads.

Chunky and muscular, they swagger along corridors, meeting the eyes of girls who seem to be magnetised by them. Wearing thick rubber-soled shoes, they bounce on the balls of their feet, calf and thigh muscles bulging against the tight fabric of their grey school trousers.

Knowing eyes and a certain charm proclaim they've 'done' it.

And would like to 'do' it again. With any available female. Anywhere. Anytime.

C'mon!

The nightmare of this new school is that I don't do Girlie; I don't do 'Let's be Best Friends'; I don't do hands-up "Me miss! Me miss!"

In my previous school, they all knew and accepted that I was an oddity. I trained. I competed. I even won medals and things. I was allowed time off school sometimes for big competitions. So I could be myself on my own terms. Little Diva, I was!

The lads didn't want to date a girl who was more muscular than them, could out run them, do more press-ups, sit-ups, lift more weights than all of them put together.

No longer prima donna, I don't know who I am. Lonely is a terrible place.

I insisted Maggie should drop me off at the end of the lane; I felt guilty that she was picking me up every morning as well as running me home from school nearly every night. On Thursdays, I would have to make my own way home, either by going to Mum's office and squatting until her home time, or catching the bus. Thursday was late night at the pet shop and Maggie worked late; Beth helped out and was paid for it.

When we first moved to Jasmine Cottage, I thought the lane was MILES long. Familiarity had gradually reduced it to about half a mile. With a heavy school bag, that was quite far enough. I was beginning to regret rejecting Maggie's offer to run me home when I heard a familiar rough engine. Coming up behind me was one of the flock of dirty, rusty white vans that roosted outside our house.

Jim the Skim had to jump out to wrestle with the sticking door; gallantly he held my elbow to help me up the high step into the passenger seat. I guessed 'the lad' was hard at work on our crumbling walls. Briefly I wondered whether Jim was one of the 'bad men' Mum had always cautioned me about. Even with the utmost straining of imagination, I couldn't quite see it; 'your little girl will be delivered safely back into the fold, mamma' I silently told my mother.

Until Jim offered me a fag, that is. Then I did become a tad uneasy. Talk about living dangerously! In case you're wondering, I refused it! I haven't done the 'my body is a temple' routine all these years to fall at the first temptation; I may not be a gymnast now, but I'm not a complete sicko!

My mother's dirty black car was starkly surrounded by the macho(?) white Transit vans. I was surprised she was home; that wasn't what we'd arranged! How dare she? Probably bunking off! But... no sign of her... I wandered through the house, expecting her to emerge from a vapour cloud of paint stripper, or covered in clotted cream paint blotches. Nor was she in the caravan, though the little kettle was hot, indicating she had recently done what she does best… brew up!

Eventually, I followed the blasting radio, the swearing and the banging and scraping sounds to – the stables.

Ducking to avoid airborne missiles, I shouted a warning and dodged my way past the stable door. Teddy was standing with his head over the field gate, highly diverted by the pantomime my insane parent appeared to have staged specially for him.

"Mum!" I shouted, and there was a brief pause in the swearing, then the sound of scraping and slithering suggested that some sheets of wood had slipped and my mum's ladylike version of swearing started again.

"What are you doing?"

Huffing and puffing to blow the house down, by the sound of it.

"What sort of Mother am I?" she bellowed above the radio which was playing a selection of rousing marches.

"D'you want me to answer that?" I yelled in time with the music.

Unidentified Flying Objects appeared to be grounded for the moment, so I crept closer and turned the radio off, as she bawled "What sort of Mother am I?" In the deafening silence, we stared at one another and burst out laughing.

"A very loud one" I suggested in a stage whisper.

She threw a bicycle tyre in my direction and it curled limply by my ankles like a battered snake.

The ground was littered with chunks of wood, tyres, oil-drums, funnels, rags, huge pieces of plywood, buckets without handles…

My elegant, stylish mother stood in the midst of the mayhem she had created, wearing filthy black jeans with ripped knees and a back pocket hanging off, an oversize T shirt bearing the faded slogan 'Pink Floyd Arena Tour' with an inflatable pink pig floating above a list of dates and venues. Hair tied back into a tight plait was covered by a red baseball cap worn backwards. Most of the spiders of the class of 2016 were having a reunion about her person; she was covered in cobwebs, stains and dust: the piece de resistance was a pair of goggles to keep muck out of her eyes.

Cover-girl for Vogue, she was NOT!

Sometimes I can't deal with my mother. Seriously batty, she does my head in! I walked away and leaned on the gate to breathe in normality with Teddy. He is Therapy About to Happen for me. By default, she is now his mother as well, but it doesn't seem to faze him at all.

Noticing a half full bottle of still water leaning against the stable wall, I unscrewed the top and thrust it into her hand.

"What is all this about then?" I asked as she tossed back her head, threw half the contents of the bottle down her throat, and let the rest dribble down her chin and over her chest.

"I was at my desk, about to go into a meeting… and I thought 'what kind of a mother am I?' and had to come straight home.

"and the answer is…?" I prompted "totally daft…? technically insane…? sweet, homely and into crocheting those little lacey mats for ladies' dressing-tables… or A.N. Other?"

"Where, I mean from whom, did you learn such sarcasm?" she nudged me and handed over the almost empty bottle.

"Mmmmmm… let me see… could it be the only parent I haven't lost?" I asked, putting my finger to my chin. "But please, enlighten me… what sort of a mother are you? As you may be aware, you are my first and only, so I'm not experienced enough to judge. Had I been a serial daughter, taking a mother here and another there… I could probably answer the question with some degree of accuracy"

"I am" she said, suddenly serious "the sort of mother who allows her only daughter to intimidate and bully her…"

"Steady on!" I cried.

"Don't mock" she said, her eyes wide and serious "I have been tiptoeing round you as if I was walking on egg-shells for months now. When I would normally say something, I've zipped my mouth. When you've been vile and rude…" (she ignored me pointing at my chest and mouthing 'Moi?' in dismay) "I've backed off and given you space…"

"Do get to the point" I said "I'm starving…"

Eyes flashing, she shouted "So when I knew you were riding that pony" whirling round, she pointed accusingly at Teddy "I didn't stop you… I never said 'but you can't ride and it isn't safe without a saddle and bridle and why don't you have some lessons first and I pretended – yes PRE-TENDED – I didn't even know what you were doing!"

"What sort of mother are you?" I demanded in a shocked voice "How could you do that?"

"Please stop being flippant, Sahara" her voice was low and urgent "this is serious. I thought… she'll come home from school and take advantage of me still being at work and she'll get on that pony with a bit of string for reins .and if she gets thrown, and smashes her head like a… like a… pumpkin (gee, thanks, Mum!) I will never forgive myself. What's more, your father will never forgive me, or gramps, or…"

"Jim the Skim, Wayne, Duane, Shane and even Electric Eric…" I suggested helpfully.

"I realise I'm wasting my breath on you" my mother was truly exasperated.

" but this is the deal… are you listening? Of course you're allowed to ride; but in future, you use a bridle. At some point soon, we get some lessons for you. You will AT ALL TIMES wear a hard hat."

"Even in bed?" I gasped.

It was too much for my poor beleaguered mother. For months she's wanted rid of The Changeling who replaced her darling daughter; longed for a good mother-daughter giggle; wished for open honest conversation. All in vain. And suddenly when she was truly in earnest about a matter of primary safety, the prodigal daughter returns, full of smart-ass remarks and flippancy. My mother exploded into laughter so vicious, she had to sit down on the dusty ground, and tears rolled down her face and plopped into the muck.

What do they call it in television? Ghosting... no, corpsing. Yup, we corpsed!

Every time we almost stopped giggling, one of us would start again. It was great. I felt as though my laughter muscles hadn't been exercised for months. My sides ached. I needed a wee. My mother held her head and howled. Later, we couldn't even have told each other what was so funny.

Faces smeared with dust, tear grooves running through the grime, eventually we helped each other to shift some of the rubbish from one place to another and finally unearthed the saddle and bridle.

Holding up the jumbled mess of dirty leather straps, I said "Is this the thing that goes on poor Teddy's head?" and Mum almost started again.

"I wouldn't..." I told her "have a clue how to even start putting this on him. The metal bit I understand... that goes in his mouth – but how d'you get the rest onto him?"

"Why don't we clean it first" she suggested "then I'll show you" but I saw her expression.

"You don't know, do you?" I shouted triumphantly.

"Maybe... maybe not" she hedged "but I know a woman who does..."

***

The last thing I expected was the arrival of Angie, the eldest of the Southward clan.

"Er…" I'd forgotten how to talk, so great was the shock "er… I thought it would be Maggie…" I mumbled.

"Sorry, no. It's me" Angie smiled, shaking Mum's hand.

"No… er… I didn't… mean… I mean…" total amnesia.

In my head, I heard Beth's voice saying "Angie's the brilliant one. She's like… wow! got so many qualifications… and she trained at the Cadre Noire!"

"I thought it would be somebody a bit more… er… humble" I stuttered.

"I can do humble" Angie was shaking her head and laughing.

"No… I mean…"

"I've brought you a present" Angie said, holding out her clenched fist

"Wow… thank you… I think" I muttered as onto my hand she dropped a small plastic box.

Turning it over and round revealed nothing except that it had a close-fitting lid, a plastic bag folded up tightly inside it, and on the outside of the lid a neat little label stating 'Northgate Diagnostics' then

Horse name…
date.…
Surname…

"Ugh?" I looked for inspiration.

"It's for a worm count" Angie explained.

"I put *worms* in it…?"

"You pack it with poo!" Angie nudged me, gently laughing.

A lightbulb moment! "Ah! *that* kind of worms! Like worming a dog?"

Yup! Off you go then… find the freshest pile you can and fill it. I'll send it off with ours from the yard. Better to do that than indiscriminately squirt wormers down his throat!"

"Why don't we have a look at your horse and this problematic bridle" Angie suggested kindly.

My mother tagged along, giving me funny questioning looks. Go away, woman!

Angie wore her dark hair pulled back into a long plait that swung down her back. She was lean and hard, fit and tanned. I notice these things since I was so obsessed with training for so long.

"People come from all over the country to work with her" I heard Beth say "She's had firsts at HOYS and Wembley and all over the place" Aaaaargh. "I'm sorry you've wasted your time" I blustered "It wasn't urgent"

"Sara!" Mum admonished.

"No… it… I mean… well…" I was bobbing up and down, almost trying to push Angie back towards her turquoise car.

Eyes rolling, Angie shook her head at me "Get out of my face, Sara" she laughed "I wanted to come. Beth's told me so much about your pony… I actually volunteered to come"

"Well… as long as you aren't expecting something that could win at… er… HOYS…" I stammered.

"Ah! I see" she said cryptically.

"What's HOYS?" Mum asked.

"Horse of the Year Show" Angie explained "Obviously my little sister has been bigging me up. It's okay, Sara, I know that there is a world beyond trophies and rosettes"

"Sorry" I mumbled. As if to make me feel better, Teddy, hearing my voice, did his wonderful Formula One impression and razzed across the field, whinnying.

How come he knows EXACTLY how to make me feel better?

Hurried rubbing at the brittle faded bridle with Neatsfoot Oil had softened it a little, but I was embarrassed to hand it over to Angie.

"Oh dear…" was all she said.

"Her horses are so beautifully turned out" I heard Beth's voice "She's produced for some of the really big names…" Aaaargh!

Business-like, she dangled the bridle in front of me, pointing out "This bit goes in his mouth, this headpiece goes behind his ears…"

I interrupted "that's the part I don't understand. When the bit is in his mouth, how d'you get that headpiece into position?"

"Ah" Angie smiled "I'm going to get all technical here, so pay attention. Those pointy sticky up bits on top of Dobbin's head are called ears. They move backwards and forwards and side to side. When you've got the bit in his mouth, you FLATTEN the ears a bit… sort of gently squidge them down… like that…" Teddy obligingly opened his mouth, then dropped his head "and pull the headpiece over. Amazingly these little pointy ear things then spring upright again"

"Ah!"

Sliding the bridle off, she handed it to me and said "Here – you have a try"

Of course it wasn't so easy. Dangling the bit in front of a closed mouth achieved nothing. Angie showed me how to slide my thumb into the corner of Teddy's mouth where there were no teeth, so that he would open it and accept the bit. I felt like I needed six hands to actually manoeuvre it all into place, but by the third attempt I was getting the hang of it. Surprisingly, I didn't lose any digits in the warm shark infested saliva in his mouth.

Angie adjusted straps and showed me which parts to buckle together, using words quite new to me; browband (is that like brow-beaten?) throat-latch, nose-band and eggbutt snaffle… scary new language! But Angie taught well and I started to understand what the pieces were all for and how they attached together.

"Very important" she said "Make a note of what holes all the buckles are fastened on so that when you pull it apart to give it a really good cleaning, you'll be able to put it back together so that it still fits Teddy" In your dreams! "Now go and put on your jods and find your hat"

I backed off in horror. "I wasn't er… thinking… of… er… riding"

"She's a brilliant teacher" Beth's voice drifted into my head "really inspirational… you know, the sort of teacher who'll be talked about for years because she knows how to get the best out of people and horses…"

By the time I came back, self-consciously pulling the back of my T-shirt down to cover my bum, Angie and Mum had put the saddle on Teddy.

"I can't…" my legs turned to jelly.

"It's okay" Angie assured me "You aren't riding on this today. It needs a bit of re-stuffing" She moved over so I could take a look. Never having examined a saddle before, I'd no idea what I was supposed to be looking at. "See" Angie rocked the saddle a little "it shouldn't do that. This pony's a bit thin at the moment. The saddle fitted him once but now he's changed shape, it would be as well to get the stuffing checked"

"I've got the number of a lady who'll come out and do it here" Mum interrupted. If she wasn't the one who was going to pay for it, I might have asked her to buzz off.

"When you've given the saddle a good clean" Angie pulled

a funny face at me "this is how it should sit. You put it on too far forward, then push it back…" she demonstrated "so that the hair all lies flat under it. Take note of how it looks… where the front comes in relation to his shoulder." She rocked it again, shifted it about on his back, then reached under his tummy for the girth. "When you fasten the girth up, be kind. Leave it loose at first, then gradually ease it up, making sure you don't pinch any hair or skin behind the buckle of the girth. Okay?"

"At this moment, yes" I said "but maybe on my own with it, I might get it wrong"

"Well, when you've had it re-stuffed, I'll come and give you a lesson… it's really important that you sit in the correct part of the saddle… but enough of that for now" Angie removed the saddle and handed it to Mum who turned and plonked it on the top rail of the gate. "Hat on!" she instructed.

I went to get my hat. And the ladder. When I came back with the step-ladder in one hand, she burst out laughing.

"Well?" I glared at her; Mum had turned away but her shoulders were shaking. "I'm usually on my own here. What else am I supposed to do?" I HATE being laughed at.

"Very sensible!" Angie commented drily "How else could you mount without a saddle?"

"I could vault on" I told her crossly "EASILY… but I didn't want to frighten him"

"Don't be cross" Angie pleaded "Horses read our moods. We don't want Teddy turning grumpy. On you get then"

Angie had told me to do my own thing – to ride Teddy as I would if she wasn't there. Easier said than done as I now had a pair of flapping reins attaching me to his mouth. Everything went wrong. I was so frightened of snagging him in the mouth that I let my reins out so loosely there was a danger he'd trip over them.

"Sara" Angie called me over. "Give him a break. How d'you expect him to feel what you're asking if your reins are like skipping ropes?"

"He's got a dirty great chunk of ugly metal in his mouth. How can I ride him without hurting him?"

"It doesn't hurt" Angie assured me "but the way you're riding will drive him mad. He's desperately trying to make contact with your hands and all you're doing is throwing away a very important means of communication. Now... shorten your reins by sliding your hands... great... well done... now – can you feel him? Think... big horse, big head, big mouth, big teeth... don't be rough, but KEEP that contact."

I hate to admit it, but it did feel better. After a few strides down the hedge-side, I could ask Teddy to turn his head one way, then the other.

Wow!

Experimenting, I rode him round the edge of the field, curving him round the corners. WOW!

Sun was gold on my face; my pony was warm beneath me. I love the smell of horse. Listening to me, his right ear was pointing back as though hearing even my breathing. Feeling my breathing, too. From the middle of my chest, I felt a huge surge of joy. I tried to control my face so that Angie wouldn't ask what I was grinning at.

In fact, I'd almost forgotten Angie was there.

With legs hanging long down my pony's sides, I revelled in the feel of my seat bones and hips following his movements. Relaxing, I felt his legs start to take longer strides, and his back swung rhythmically. As soon as that happened, I felt so much more comfortable. It was like being molten liquid flowing into his movement.

As always, I asked for changes of pace; halt, walk on,

turn, go onto a circle, halt… and it all felt so much easier with the reins to back up my body aids.

When I asked for canter, it was so beautiful and flowing and easy that I felt as though I might weep with joy.

***

Rewarded with a thick section of hay, Teddy was contentedly munching in his paddock. Lucky him. My only reward was to be dispatched urgently to do my homework. The only table was in the Midget-Van, so I rigged up a table-lamp and settled myself down with pristine exercise books - which wouldn't be that way for long!

Outside, a thrush was serenading his mate with quite sublime long lyrical repeating musical phrases. I had the itsy-bitsy window open behind me and a scented breeze sweetened the air.

"Maggie will be absolutely sick" I heard Angie say. Like Teddy, my ears pricked. "She was going to come – she looks on Sara as 'hers' – but had forgotten she was delivering some dog food to her best friend and that's always a long job – that is, if she makes it home at all"

Ask why Maggie will be sick, Mum. Ask.

"Why will Maggie be sick?" Mum asked. There was a sound of chairs being moved; obviously they were going to sit outside and have a drink or something.

Angie let out a huge sigh, then said "Sara is the most exciting rider I've met for years"

WHAT?

"What? WHAT?" gasped my gobsmacked parent.

"Didn't you realise?"

"Realise… What exactly?"

"I couldn't believe it when she said she's only been riding for a few weeks" Angie said "and even more, I couldn't believe it when she insisted she's never had any lessons"

"Is she good?" Mum asked.

Angie made a mock-sobbing noise. "Good? Good doesn't even come into it"

Oh come on! Don't be stupid!

"Oh come on" said the parent "it's just... er... beginner's luck or something"

"No. NO. NO!" Angie insisted "For heaven's sake, I've been teaching for years. We used to have a riding school. Seriously... I have never seen a novice – novice and self taught – rider with such a natural talent"

There you go, Dad, you disbeliever who thought I was rubbish at everything... come and talk to this lady. Did you get that... she said 'natural talent'

"You will have a drink, won't you?" That's my mum! Always playing for time.

She likes to think things through.

"I can't be late; I'm on yard duty tonight and have all the horses to feed" Angie said "but we do need to talk about this"

The page before me was blank. Ugh! What was the stupid essay about? What subject was it, even? My mum was not the only one suffering from gobsmack!

More shifting of chairs and clinking of glasses. Mum muttered something about it being non-alcoholic wine... white or red... or tea, coffee?

Get on with it, will you; how can I settle to homework until I know what this is all about?

A couple of blackbirds rustled in the undergrowth; wrap-around 3D sound of birds preparing for a night of passion.

"So..." Mum began "give it to me in short words that a total idiot could understand"

"Sara could be a fantastic rider" Angie said, putting her glass down on the table "she's got it all - incredible balance... she's athletic, supple..."

"That'll be all the gymnastics. You know she's been training for years?" Mum interrupted. Here we go; proud mother is going to big it up. "There was talk of her making it to the Commonwealth Games… possibly even… well… I don't know…"

"What made her good at gymnastics is probably what makes her a good rider" Angie said "the balance, fitness, body shape… all that… BUT lots of riders have that, either naturally or by working hard at it. What makes Sara different and special (she said I'm SPECIAL. Tell that to your stick-insect pregnant girl-friend, Dad) is an intuitive understanding about what riding is all about. Some riders – some good riders never, ever get that."

"What's so special? She's only been riding a few weeks? She can't even trot yet" Mum protested.

"She uses her breathing and her diaphragm. She feels all that's going on in her own body and in the horses. Instinctively she knows how to 'get him going' – even without a saddle." Angie paused "I'm really scared that people are going to spoil her… tell her to do this and that…" there was a clinking of glasses and bottle. In the stillness a woodpigeon cooed softly.

"I want to be her teacher" Angie finished in a rush. "Please… let me…"

Chapter 10

By the time Angie drove away home, it was quite dark. Not a great deal had been achieved in the homework department, but I hoped I'd done enough to keep the teachers happy. I shall just have to play the 'new girl; still settling in' card if challenged.

Very hard to keep your mind on the American Civil War and conjugating French verbs when your brain is in overdrive.

What on earth is Angie on? I've never had a riding lesson; I've never read a book on riding; never watched documentaries or sat in on a lesson. Actually, it seems I'm just a huge fraud who happened to get it right while Angie was watching. Yeah, I sort of get the stuff about balance and flexibility – and even the diaphragm bit. But does that make a rider (or even, in the style of Willy Shakes 'doth that a rider make?')

Tossing about on my mattress on the floor in my empty shell of a bedroom, I watched the time reflected onto the ceiling from my alarm clock. When I'd watched several hours appearing on the sloping roof, I crawled across the floor to the pile of clothes laughingly called a 'wardrobe', selected a grotty track suit to throw on over my 'jamas, stuffed my feet into a pair of trainers and let myself out of the house. Mum still sleeps in the dwarf shack and wouldn't hear me unless I pushed her caravan over as I passed.

Beautifully soft and mild, the night wasn't particularly dark, though it amazes me to live here and be so immersed in silence and darkness. There are no streetlights down the lane, although one or two of the posh houses have armour-ies of security lights. At this witching hour, all lights are sleeping unless some villain selects the house with the swim-ming pool for raping and pillaging – though it's more likely to be a safer pastime like burglary – when all the lights will blind him into submission.

Blossom perfumed the night air. A few stars loitered in the velvet darkness behind gently moving clouds. Picking my way carefully through the debris on the lawn, I headed towards Teddy's field. Dew drenched my trainers. When I touched the gate into the paddock, it was damp.

Apart from a few night creatures scurrying through dried foliage in the hedge-bottoms, nothing stirred. "Teddy" I called softly, expecting his usual winged gallop. Nothing. My eyes strained to see him through the gloom. I expected at least a dark profile, a lumpen dark mass. A friendly shout.

Alarm started to tighten my muscles. Had we shut the gate properly? How could he have escaped? Can he jump? If so, can he jump a five-barred gate? If so, why didn't he jump out last winter when he was lonely and almost starving? Stolen?

Oh no! I began to run towards the gate into the orchard, wondering if the grass in there had lured him into escapology.

And almost fell over him. His excited little greeting suggested I'd woken him up. A dark hump on the ground, I worked out his back legs were tucked neatly under his stomach and his front legs stretched out before him. Bless! I'd never seen a horse lying down before – at least only on statues or in pictures.

I stroked his face, then sank down beside him, fitting myself against his side.

Scientific break here; Horses don't actually lie down very much. Some don't lie down at all, but sleep standing up. They have a special Thing that locks their legs so they don't crumple in a heap as they relax. Clever, huh? The reason they don't lie down for long is that they are heavy and their own weight would crush their lungs. If a horse needs an operation, the vet has to work really fast to bring it round and haul it onto its feet as quickly as possible so it won't develop lung complaints.

So if you have a pony and think of him snuggled down in his jim-jams in a lovely straw bed, catching zeds all the time you're in bed – think again! He'll be up and down, mooching around his stable, watching the night sky, eating his bedding, meditating or doing whatever horses do when left for long periods. He will NOT be lying down asleep.

I'm telling you all this in case you ever have an elephant for a pet, because the same thing applies there. Probably giraffes as well.

At that time, I'd never seen a horse rising from recumbent (*lying down!*). It's pretty messy and ungainly. Had I known this, I would have made sure I didn't fall asleep leaning against him. But hey! too late now!

How he managed to pull himself out from under me, dig his hooves into the ground in order to lever himself up and sort out all four legs and a heavy head without doing me some permanent damage, I shall never know. It will remain one of the Great Unanswered Questions of all time – did he try very hard not to fracture several of my bones and avoid stomping half-a-ton of horsemeat on the delicate muscle on my thigh? Or was I very, very lucky?

Either way, when I was woken by the pesky birds coughing up phlegm as a warm-up exercise for the Dawn Chorus, I was lying in the middle of a very damp field and my Gallant

Steed was stuffing his face with grass, totally ignoring me. I crept onto my cold mattress in my chilly empty bedroom and tumbled deep into sleep at just about the time the alarm was thinking 'will I or won't I?' Of course, it did, rudely. My eyelids were still gunged together when Maggie and Beth came to pick me up for school.

Grunting at Beth was all I could manage. I get it now, this grunting thing. It's about lack of sleep as much as lack of social skills.

"Bog off" was the most animated and articulate I could be all the way to school.

***

Loads of things happened in the days that followed.

First I found my misplaced mobile phone... don't ask!

There were several missed calls, most of them from my ex-father. Boring. Boring... Also:

Text 1:

> Hope yr nu scool is brill & betr than old 1.
> Miss u lots. Gaz ast me out!!!! Kim

Bit of a shock here: how fickle am I? I've become so involved in my new life that I had to press rewind to remember who Kim is. Still don't know who Gaz is – some lad she's had the hots for, no doubt. Then again, knowing Kim, he could be some dude who just smiled at her once and she thinks she's in.

DELETE.

Text 2:

> Darling, please answer my calls. I know you must be hurting, but I AM still your father. We can work this out. Love you, Dad.

DELETE

Text 3:
Hope yr 1st day @ new school is great – or at least
tolerable. Lets meet up @ ½ term. U gon so quiet on
me. I wanna know wotz hapnin. Miss u. Zoe

Guilt creeps up on me. I've shut them all out. Must try
harder. Will phone Zoe tonight.

Text 4:
U swotty cow. Wot did u do to impress Anj so? Thort
u cdn't ride? She RAVED abt u. Explain yrself. Beth

Ouch! I'm going to get some stick. And I still don't know
what I'm doing to impress. Hey-ho… some have got it,
some haven't!

Hope Beth doesn't hate me because I'm a swotty cow.

***

Sometime in that week, the lady saddle-fitter turned up to
stuff Teddy's saddle. Shock! Horror ! My mother sat on my
pony to see if the stuffing worked.

MY PONY!

How Dare She?

A lesson was arranged for Saturday, when Angie would
come to see how I coped with a saddle.

"Teacher's pet!" Beth taunted.

"You're just jealous" was my rather lame response.

"Definitely NOT!" she said, with so much emphasis that
I began to worry about Angie as a Mad Sadistic Instructor.

Teddy and I practised our bridle and rein skills like mad.
Just in case!

Chapter 11

Seeing him standing there as I came out of school was – well
- unbelievable. Brain went into a total nose-dive, leaving
nothing but sheer physical reaction and a high-pitched buzz-
ing in my head. Rigid, I stopped dead. Beth, who was coming up somewhere behind me, but talking to Hayley, ran into
the back of me.

"Shift" she laughed, pushing at my shoulders. My legs had
turned to jelly; there was no question of shifting. I felt as
though my eyes had popped out of my head, and my hair
seemed to be standing on end (actually, in retrospect, the
sort of style I used to spend hours spiking in front of a mirror!).

Real, he stood there as my heart turned somersaults and it
felt as though electrical shocks were running up my body
from my feet.

"Sara…?" Beth was now peering into my face. I couldn't
speak, but weird choking sounds made my throat jump and
gag.

For months, he'd been a thing in my imagination; I'd
thought he was still real, but he wasn't. He'd become…
what? a puppet?… a cardboard cut-out?… a character from
a bad Gothic novel? I hadn't FELT his reality for so long

that it was a shock to see him alive, visible, human.

"Sara...? you okay...?" Beth's face loomed before me in a surreal dream-like way, but I couldn't quite focus on her. Beyond her he stood waiting. Slowly, Beth turned her head and followed the direction of my gaze.

"Is it your dad?" she asked, but I couldn't answer. For a moment I glimpsed her panic; sensed that she felt out of her depth, but his eyes were drawing me to him, his arms opening wide, welcoming.

Between my father and I, dozens of uniformed kids ambled and pushed and swerved. It seemed as though his eyes held mine even when blocked by a passing head or shoulders. Beth had disappeared. My tongue was glued to the roof of my mouth. Across the distance, I could see his mouth forming the shape of my name – could hear his voice in my head, saying the vowels of my name.

Had I been waiting for him?

Had I hungered for him, even while hating him?

Dream-like, the air between us felt charged with electricity. My father.

Daddy.

Part of me; an integral part of my history.

Our blood, flesh, DNA, heritage so interwoven that we should recognise each other on a subliminal level.

"Sahara..." I could hear him across a vast landscape. Arms dangling by my sides, I waited for the red mist to clear from my brain.

Some feeling was creeping back through the numbness. My father...

The man who rejected all the effort I put into trying to make him proud of me, who started an affair with – whatever-her-name is... and started a new baby inside her... as though I wasn't the Right One... wasn't enough...

He wanted a better model; a better model than Mum, too. Lying, cheating, breaking promises…

Shaking my head like a mad dog, I felt all the rage of the last few months pulsing into my head with every memory of betrayal.

"Sahara…" arms held wide, calling me into them.

"No" my voice struggled free from the debris blocking my throat.

Beth and Maggie drifted into the dream then, their eyes wide with fear, faces pale. "Sara!" Maggie spoke sharply, to penetrate the fog.

"No" I said again, but really to my father.

"Come home, Sara" Beth urged.

Across a wilderness, he was still holding my eyes, his thoughts calling…

"No!" I shouted.

Maggie planted herself directly in front of me, blocking my view of him, peered into my face and said loudly, distinctly "Sara. Do you want to go with that man? Do you want to talk to him?"

Several aeons passed while my nauseous brain struggled to interpret her question.

How could he have left me? If he loved me, how could he?

"No! No!" I shouted.

Then it got messy. My father must have sensed that Maggie was winning and covered the ground between us. I could smell his familiar after-shave, see a pulse in his neck. Did he always have crooked teeth, my imbecile brain wondered.

To my right, Beth had dragged my school-bag off my shoulder and rummaged through it for my mobile phone.

"Sahara" my father spoke, his voice rich with emotion.

"We don't know what to do" Beth gabbled into my phone.

"Come with me… somewhere we can talk…" he pleaded

"I've missed you so"

A horrible hissing sound filled my head; maybe it was the venomous sound of that snake of a woman he'd run off with...

"take her home with us...?" Beth's voice cut in.

"Sara" Maggie stared into my eyes insistently "What do you want to do?"

"Come with me" my father pleaded, and roughly snapped at Maggie "She's MY daughter... you get out of it... this is nothing to do with you..."

The hissing stopped; the red mist cleared.

My brain felt cold and clear.

"Go to your new woman" I told him "you threw me away..."

"Not YOU!" he shouted.

Somewhere deep in the confusion, I almost laughed, but it became a choking sound as all the things I'd wanted to say to him for so long jostled to be first out.

"Go AWAY!" I shouted "There is no forgiveness here for you" and turned, dragging Maggie with me.

Straightening my back, I dredged up all my gymnastic training – the ability to walk tall and dignified even when your world has just crashed. Toe then heel, toe then heel... putting distance between me and my father.

He didn't follow. Beth kept glancing over her shoulder and I could gauge from her breathing that with each glance, she felt safer.

At some point, the gymnastic training let me down and my knees buckled, but by then we were close to Maggie's Land Rover and between them, they hoisted me up – an elbow each – and in silence squashed me up and into the bench seat between them.

"So that's your dad, huh" said Beth flippantly, trying to

lighten the mood.

"No" I said, swallowing hard to stem a tsunami of tears "that's my ex-dad"

***

Arriving home was quite an experience. Bizarre changed into Burlesque. I was aroused out of my lethargy by the sight of a vehicle parked alongside the grown-up requisite (rusty) white vans. Is it a car; is it a van; is it a glorified motor-bike? Hmmm. Colourful, it was, smeared with slogans, flowers, rainbows, go-faster stripes.

"Oh dear" said my parent.

"What?" for the first time in several hours, my voice had a ring of familiarity. Was that echo my Inner Monster rearing its battered head?

"Er... ooops!"

"Do tell"

"Um. Well... Wayne has this mate. He's a second year decorating apprentice. And... er..."

"You're employing the person who decorated that – vehicle – to paint our house?" I asked incredulously.

"Um... more precisely... er... your bedroom"

Was that horrendous scream inside my head or out loud? "You're kidding?"

"Remember. If it's awful, it's only emulsion; we can always paint over it" she said reasonably.

"Not if it's all over your carefully sanded floorboards... and the windowsills... and the stripped pine doors..." even to me, my voice sounded nasty.

"He is a SECOND year student"

Exhausted, I really couldn't fight any more. "Okay... but you get a proper decorator in to repaint if necessary"

"Of course" I could see she had her fingers crossed behind her back as she slithered out of the car.

Lads. Huh! Oh purleez! Wayne laid claim to me. He'd never spoken more than three sentences to me before, but suddenly he was chatty and flirty; marking his territory in his own way. They were in my bedroom so I couldn't even change out of school uniform. Wayne snivelled and grovelled and his eyes pleaded with me to make it look like we were mates. So I deliberately flirted with the other spotty 'erbert, just because I could! He was called Joe and had long hair. Most importantly, he'd already applied one coat of clotted cream paint to the ceiling and it looked good. Wayne, more used to flinging plaster around, was rollering paint onto one of the walls. And himself. And his Doc Martens.

I left them to it. My bones felt weary; my head ached.

Pulling an old track-suit top on over my school clothes, I grabbed a bottle of water and scooted out to the field.

Teddy rushed to meet me, chunnering loudly. Emitting a huge sigh, I breathed in the wonderful horse-ness of him and immediately felt better. He is so SANE. All else is madness (including me!)

What a farce! Feeling quite spaced out, I tried to remember my father, but he'd receded again into a cartoon or an inflatable. No longer real, I couldn't quite recall why I'd freaked out so.

And then... Oh NO! Suddenly remembering... I'll never live it down! Maggie and Beth took me home and sat me down in their kitchen. Somebody plonked a blue mug of tea in front of me; the mug had a weird grinning cat on it. There were a lot of things going on there. I was so out of it, I don't know what happened. People came and went. I'm not daft or deaf; I saw the meaningful looks and heard the whispered conversations outside the room. What did I do? Sat at their kitchen table, pulled open my school bag for my books... and started doing homework!

Oh no!

Beth will tell everyone; she was joking about it at the time but I was too spaced out to understand. Homework? at a time like that?

Help!

When Mum came for me, Maggie took her outside and obviously gave her a blow-by-blow account of what had happened. Maybe she coloured it with her own imaginings. She must have wondered what the hell was going on.

Buzz-word of the day: SHOCK.

I am, according to everyone from the insane cat on my mug of tea to my distressed parent, in shock.

***

One thing I do know – in Gymnastics, you learn to be tough. Really tough. Crash and burn, get up, try again. Gymnasts are always covered in bruises. We dance on this ridiculously narrow beam, then fling ourselves about on it, leap into the air and turn, flip, revolve. And expect to land on it every time!

We swing up and over a bar so high we have to be hoisted onto it; do handstands on it, fling ourselves here and there, leave loose. We fly and... if we're lucky, catch the lower bar; if not, we splatter ourselves onto the mats, get up and start again.

Tough, we train ourselves not to blub, not to say Ouchouchouch as tears spring to our eyes. Arnica is consumed in vast quantities to ease the bruising; Rhus Tox to combat stiffness; if we are lucky, we may be awarded the heavy hands of the club physiotherapist – a fate worse than suffering in silence.

We do not cry.

We do not have tantrums (*at least not in public*).

We cheer for team-mates who may have just pipped us to medal position.

We are Ladies of Steel; well 'ard!

So it's surprising that I have recently learned how to cry; and boy! am I practising this new found skill!

I don't know about competing for England; I could weep for England.

On my first day at new school, I caught sight of myself in the mirror in the girls' toilets. What a shock! Remember, we're living on a building site here

and a mirror would be an extravagance, a luxury and a frippery sure to be smashed by the first length of wood pushed into the house. This person in the mirror was not me; it was softer. If not plumper, it was slightly less gaunt. Hard, taut muscles had relaxed; razor-sharp cheek bones looked more rounded. And my hair! O wow! I haven't touched it for weeks; just forgot that it needed trimming to keep the jaggy 'urchin' cut which could so easily be spiked into a lethal weapon. Now, it's longer, curling a bit, falling round my face.

Conceited I may be, but I have to confess, I looked prettier.

So along with a softer profile, I have the insides of a jelly.

Iron Maiden no more. I have become a wuss.

That's probably what Teddy thought as I draped myself over him and staunched my tears with his mane. Again!

Bless him! He stood there like a saturated handkerchief as I bubbled and wobbled and howled out my pain. 'Oh-oh!' he probably thinks as he sees my bleary, teary face approaching, 'bath-time again!'

Bored with the drama queen act, Teddy moved gently away, grazing. With one arm draped over his back, I followed, enjoying the smell of him, the closeness, the minute movements of his body fluids, muscles, tendons, ligaments, his tail-swishing.

From my bedroom came a horrific continual blast of heavy-metal music. Great to have my room painted… but I hoped they weren't having secret fantasies as they did it.

Birds were beginning their evensong. The sky had a smudged, bruised look about it that could mean rain later. Teddy and I moved as one in search of odd succulent blades of grass.

One of my mother's Grumpy Old Woman complaints is about people who talk too loudly into their mobile phones – especially people who shout and walk about - especially people who holler and walk about AND say things like "I've just got on the train" or "I'm walking from the station" or "I'm coming in through the front door…"

So it was with surprise that I heard her shouting into her mobile and walking up and down the garden path as she did so.

"I can't understand what you hoped to achieve…"

"Didn't you realise? I mean, can't you see that it was the worst thing you could have done…?"

Obviously my ex-father was on the other end.

I'll put it this way: my mother was not in her long floaty dress, gathering twee little bunches of wild flowers, singing soppy old ballads sort of mood.

Think — Cruella de Ville in a foul and icy mood.

Think — an axe murderer wondering in whose head she left her axe embedded.

Think — well… I'm sure you get the picture.

"… poisoning her mind against you? You don't need me to do that! You're doing a perfectly good job all by yourself…"

"… give her some space… you're not exactly her favourite person at the moment…"

"… custody? You're mad! Why would she want to come and live with you?"

CUSTODY   ???????

Chapter 12

Taken as a whole, that was one seriously weird week.

One thing I really enjoyed though, was arriving home each evening to find surprises. Like Electric Eric had given us lights and sockets in every room.

Like the New Kid on The Block had arrived in the form of a kitchen fitter. Oh yippee!

Like Jim and his trusty squire had finished all the plastering and were hard at work tiling the bathroom. One day soon we shall be able to have showers.

When all the proper workmen rattled away up the lane to their wives and unfinished jobs in their own homes, down the lane came the Lurv-Machine carrying Wayne and Joe. Surprisingly they were turning out to be real assets; despite playing Metallica at ear-splitting decibels! Neat, tidy and hard-working (maybe because Mum was paying them per wall or ceiling!) they had finished my TWO rooms (!) and were hard at work on Mum's lavender walls. Some urgency here, as she wanted it habitable by the weekend when (hooray!) her sister Jen was coming to stay.

"Jen has such a good eye" my mother said at frequent intervals, making me visualise her as that one-eyed Cyclops dude from Greek mythology. "She can take you shopping on Saturday and help you choose fabrics and accessories for your room"

"S"

"What?"

"RoomZ" I corrected. "Two RoomZ"

"Yesyesyes...your two rooms" Mum's voice was snidey. "Meanwhile, Jen and I will have to share my one room"

"Only for the weekend"

"Well... you can share your room with Wayne as I've asked him to stay over and paint the lounge"

Speechless, I did a fair goldfish impression, until I saw the evil gleam in her eye.

"Anyway" I said "I can't do Saturday. I'm having a lesson with Angie"

"That's not til late afternoon. You and Jen can go and have girlie bonding time in the morning, then I'll drag her round the same shops in the afternoon, helping me to choose fabrics for my room"

Sometimes, I think my mother is quite childish. But that's what she wants me to think.

Home time had become an ordeal since That Man had stalked me.

I noticed that Beth abandoned her friends and made it seem quite natural to walk out of school with me. Maggie would be waiting at the school gate. Previously, she had sat in the car wherever she could find space to park, and wait for us to find her. Now her anxious face would be searching for us among the hordes of cloned kids. So serious was the situation that Beth didn't tease her or complain that we weren't toddlers to be met at the gate and held by the hand until we reached the safety of the Defender.

My mother, the Rottweiler, must have frightened him off. He didn't re-appear. I never asked her what he had said about Custody; I think I was too scared to hear. My reaction would have been HE CANNOT BE SERIOUS! I mean, why would I want to live with him? He's a cad, as my nan would say. As for living with the Toxic New Model... purleez. I'd rather frolic naked in a freezing market. At some point in this horrid past year, he'd said something like "I thought you always wanted a brother or sister..."

Duh! "Preferably from the same parents" I'd shouted at him "not from some tart you've picked up and dumped us for..."

I don't do the 'all men are bastards' line, but my father does not give me hope that they aren't.

Meanwhile... back at the ranch...

Teddy and I have had some lovely walks. Feeling safe to lead him out with the bridle for control, I've been getting up with the flippin' squawking birds at the 'crack of dawn' and taking him up the lane and back before all the BMWs and Range Rovers start the school run. Bless him; his neat little ears are always pricked up in curiosity and interest and he's a joy to spend time with. Unlike most people I know.

Schedule for the weekend: Jen is coming on Friday and staying until Sunday. Lots of shopping!

Lesson with Angie on Saturday afternoon. Sunday morning, Beth is coming to help clear all the unwanted rubbish out of the stable and tack-room.

And, as almost a permanent fixture (though NOT in my bedroom), Wayne will be wielding a paint roller. Urgent now as the carpet fitter is coming next week.

Hallelujah!

Saturday afternoon; my lesson with Angie was not a great success. It wasn't Angie who was the problem, but the dratted saddle. How does anybody manage to ride on a hard slippery instrument of torture like that.

Only one good thing about it: I didn't feel like my wellies were going to slip off my feet, as the stirrups held them on.

When I'm bareback, I can feel every twitch and flexion of Teddy's muscles beneath me. It's easy to mould myself to him; to be moved by his movement.

Perched on the ridiculously hard leather thing, it was all I could do to stay put, let alone be at one with my horse.

I muttered, I cursed.

Angie coaxed and promised it would get better. I demanded to be allowed to ride without the wretched thing. She swore I would work through it and be a better rider with it. I slithered about, grumbled that my stirrups were too short. Or too long. Felt as though my ankles were being forced into an unnatural angle which hurt.

Angie laughed and said I looked like a proper rider at last. Teddy bounced along with his ears twitching and his back hollow. I threw a hissy-fit and said I didn't want a lesson. In fact, didn't EVER want to ride EVER again.

Exasperated, at last Angie said crossly "Okay. Get off then. Lesson over"

"Oh"

She turned and stomped away, and I felt awful because she was giving me lessons for free, and I was being a miserable sod. My Inner Monster was on top form; surprising, as he's been fairly placid lately.

Waving her arms around and speaking loudly, Angie complained to my mother that I was a quitter and she was going home.

Ouch!

Shame-faced, I kept Teddy on a large circle and really concentrated on what he was doing rather than what I was doing. The saddle started to feel marginally less inhospitable. In fact… yes, it did sort-of keep me in the correct place on his back... and... well... yes... the stirrups did help me to ride lighter... and oh well...

Teddy dropped his head and his back-end began to swing more. I squeezed with my legs and his stride grew longer. Somehow, now that I'd stopped focussing on the saddle, it was working better.

Angie was still standing at the gate, pretending not to be taking any notice, but I kept catching her eye and knew she was very aware of what I was doing.

All pretty boring stuff... walk, halt, walk, lengthen stride, check, etc. Then I asked for trot; bear in mind I don't do trot. Bareback, I was slithering all over the place and being jolted up through my spine and all my guts were being churned up.

Ah-ha!

Bliss!

Joy!

Trot was... not only possible but... really, honestly... enjoyable.

It took a few strides of bumping up and down, almost damaging my coccyx on the hard saddle before I got it. Embarrassed that I had actually thought I could ride... I was finding all over again that I hadn't a clue!

I kept losing the rhythm, or feeling that he had shot out from under me. Or I bounced an extra stride, or slid sideways or...

Well... anything that could go wrong, did. And WOW, was it tiring!

Me, fit! NOT!

Me, exhausted after a few minutes.

Wander about a bit, halt, walk, canter a circle. Walk. Try another trot; I was totally inside my own head as I trained my body to respond in the way that felt most comfortable for me, but also seemed to make Teddy happier. When happy, his neck curved, and he didn't have his pointy ears stuck up my nostrils, and he felt sort-of light. Like a bike that's been well-oiled.

Change direction. Walk, canter, try to slow down smoothly from canter to trot.

Hmmm. Not very good. Try to get a good smooth change from trot to canter... better...

"That's enough for today" Angie said "Teddy isn't very fit yet".

"Thought you'd gone home" I muttered sourly.

"I needed a lesson" she laughed. "You gave it to me. Sorry! I should have known you're a little madam who needs to work things out for herself"

Honestly, you can't get good instructors these days, can you!

Sunday was a brilliant day, and I had more fun than I've had in years. I kept getting quite disorientated by hearing this loud laughter – mine. Apart from the mad moment in the stable with my mother the other day I can't remember when I last had a really good belly-laugh. It seems that my Inner Monster has nearly wiped out the desire to laugh.

In fact, my past feels like a dream. I struggle to recall faces and places. I remember the slog and more slog of Gymnastics; how could I have become so addicted to a sport which no longer gave me any pleasure. Odd bright moments would glimmer through – the memory of actually managing a double somersault or winning a medal or a beautiful flowing tumble at the end of Floor. Apart from that, it was hard work; not many laughs there.

Then...That Man! Like some Shape-Shifter, he'd become a cold stranger who didn't care when he hurt his family. His heart had shunted itself off to a new life with his new love, and even before that ghastly day when he'd moved out, it was like living with a grey thing. Months of hurting had drained both me and Mum. Bitter, I refused to listen to anything she said. When we should have been clinging together, I turned into the brat from hell and made things far worse for her.

One day, when I REALLY mean it, I'll apologise to her. At the moment. I'm never sure when that beastly Inner Monster will decide to have his spiteful fun; I tread carefully.

Having my aunty Jen staying with us was like taking a brisk walk in a bracing wind. Mum shed at least ten years. I've never seen her so frivolous and such fun since the day… well, when she found out about my ex-father's double life. Copious amounts of booze were consumed on Saturday night. NOT by me, of course; I've moved on from the My Body Is a Temple phase, but still don't want to poison my cells. NOT that I'd be allowed, you understand. My mum can be scatty, but she's not totally stupid.

Sunday was late starting as my elderly relatives were too hung over to greet the dawn. Also, I was waiting for Beth to ride over from Oak Tree on Zeb, and knew she wouldn't arrive before the birds had finished practising their discords. Having some time, I took the bull by the horns, or in this case, the horse by the reins, mounted and rode Teddy up the lane and back. It was fantastic! Riding out feels quite different from endless circles in the field.

Memo to self: buy a detailed large-scale map of this area to locate bridle-paths and tracks. I could really get into this riding lark – known in the trade as 'hacking out'.

Sitting in the sun on a white plastic chair, I waited for the minions to unstick their eyelids and put in an appearance. Beth made it first; neat little clip clops coming down the lane. Teddy whizzed round in circles of excitement as he saw Zeb through the hedge.

Beth explained that you can't just put two strange horses in a field together or they'll kick each other to bits, jump out or, at the very least, charge round so much that they'll churn up the field to the consistency of our lawn. So Zeb was untacked and turned out in the orchard, while Teddy stood wistfully at the gate, chunnering. Occasionally, when Zeb condescended to throw a few words of comfort to him, they squealed at each other and lashed out with their front legs. "This is the way it is" Beth said, matter-of-factly. "You NEVER turn them out together straight away unless you want a massive vets bill! After a few days, they'll have worked out the pecking order and should settle down"

"Poor Teddy won't have that chance" I remarked. "I feel really guilty because he's obviously lonely"

"Yeah… but compared to his life before you came here, this is luxury" Beth said "and look at him… he's a different horse. He's put on weight, but not too much; and his coat shines… and he looks so much happier…"

I was feeling very smug at this lavish praise, until she said "Angie called you a little madam, didn't she?" and laughed wickedly.

"I was!"

"It did her good" Beth said "Normally people bow and scrape and do whatever she says because she's got some sort of reputation as a teacher. I think she was quite shocked!"

"I feel really bad!"

"Don't!" Beth laughed "Afterwards, she said it had done her good… she forgets that some people need a different style of teaching. I think you're a challenge!"

"Ouch!" I said "I'm sure she's a brill teacher. It's just… well, I need to get my head round things. I don't want to be a puppet, reacting rather than knowing"

"You are seriously eccentric" Beth shook her head.

"Moi? Why?" I was amazed.

"You make life so… er… complicated; so difficult. You are SO the opposite of laid-back"

"Am I really?"

Her dark hair glinted blue in the sun as she shook her head in puzzlement "You mean, you don't know this?" she asked.

"Erm… well… No!"

"That's a sure sign that you are WELL deranged!"

Murmurings from the house then as Mum and Jen came out carrying mugs of strong coffee, and very sheepish expressions.

"Behold the lambs" I told Beth. "Last night, they were 'drinking, carousing and living a life of sin. The whole area must have been kept awake by their singing and laughing. It's a good thing we're well away from civilisation or they'd have been trying to pull. Poor Ned what's-his-name at the next farm could have been a victim"

"Yeah, right!" Mum laughed. "He's very sweet, but hardly the stuff that heroes are made of"

"You wanna hero?" Jen giggled "I'd just settle for a MAN!"

"I've moved to the country for the healthy smell of cow-muck on a farmer's clothes; or maybe someone like Lady Chatterley's gamekeeper"

"No… Mister Darcy for me! Especially with the fortune" Jen said.

"You've got a man!" I told her indignantly.

"Doesn't stop me from window shopping" she giggled.

"We're going to make a start on the stable" I was starting to feel embarrassed in front of Beth by these dippy relatives. "Drink lots of coffee, then see if you can find your way down the garden"

This was the Plan: Mum and Jen would start chucking rubbish into one of the builders' skips. This way, they hoped to clear a space in the biggest shed. Which we would then fill! Simple; logical.

I won't bore you with every oil drum, funnel, bit of string, hunk of wood, sheet of plywood etcetera that we shifted. Nor by describing in detail how we became festooned with spiders' webs onto which every dead fly, wasp, and a selection of dried mice droppings then clung. A pretty sight it was not!

With the two grown-ups (allegedly) behaving like kids, we worked hard at being serious. It actually did matter to us; we wanted to play ponies properly, with stables and a tack room and lots of horsey things around. Mum and Jen were intent on giving their Inner Children a jolly good playtime and stuff hard labour.

Beth and I rolled our eyes in exasperation, and told them off when they rolled on the ground crying with laughter. Really – there was nothing particularly funny; it was just one of those days when the most trivial incident started them off again. Sometimes we couldn't help ourselves, and joined in, but in an indulgent way like stiff parents trying to Be Fun.

Dragging and carrying and barrowing all the stuff my mum and aunt had jammed into the stables only a few weeks before, we made a mess of flower-beds, gravel pathways and what was left of the lawn. We were not helped by my adolescent mother running amok, whooping and leaping over heavy items we were trying to carry. At last, though, Beth and I dumped the final load of wheels, buckets, broken chairs, rotted parasols, and their own load of dead insects, cobwebs and the inevitable mice pellets, at the feet of my relatives who, by this time, had settled down with their feet up and glasses of cordial in hand.

"All yours" I told them, smugly, dusting my hands together.

"Don't wanna do it!" Jen laughed.

"Tough!"

"She's mean" Jen told my mother.

"I know" Mum laughed "... a real termagant"

"... or is it a curmudgeon?"

"No, that's a miser"

"She could be that as well" they nodded their heads at each other, in such a way that I wondered whether their cordial had been laced with something a little stronger.

Whatever, I didn't want Beth to have more ammunition; she thinks I'm seriously odd as it is. "Let's go and get a drink" I suggested, not liking the expression in her eyes; obviously she was storing up all this stuff to tease me with should I step out of line. "... then you can give me a lesson in stable management"

Once we had cleared away all the junk from the inside and outside of the stables... wow!... I have a stable block! It looked like a picture out of a book. "Great!" Beth enthused.

"Mine" I said in wonder.

All wooden (tongue and groove, I'm told) with felted roofs, there were two loose boxes and a tack room. Notice, I'm sparing you from 'the wooden roomy thing and horse's bedroom' ignorance, because now I know terms like loose box and tack room. When we swept out the last of the dust and debris from the stables, we found they had rubber matting on the floor. (Duh?!) Good job Beth knows her stuff. Yeh, yeh, yeh... keeps hocks from capping (?), saves on bedding bla-di-bla. Goody for me!

Stable block then: two loose boxes, according to Beth 'twelvebitwelve'; in old money, that's a space big enough for a horse to have plenty of room to wander about, lie down, stand up and do whatever horse's do in the privacy of their own bedrooms.

We swept, brushed down cobwebs and accumulated dust,

disinfected the floors and cleaned the windows. Lurvly!

Then we carried everything out of the tack room and laid it out on the concrete area of the stable yard. If you have a pony, you'll know how much stuff one 'needs' for it. Personally, I'm still getting my head round this!

I do understand saddle, bridle and stuff to clean them with. A couple of brushes, buckets. Yup! All seems logical... but boxes full of leather straps of all shades and shapes? rugs, more rugs, even more rugs? seven haynets? Long whips, short whips, dressage whip, schooling whip, lungeing whip? Purleez! am I to understand that we are going to whip this poor equine into submission? Saddle cloths, numnahs, exercise sheets?

Help!

What Are They All For?

Does my pony really need all this stuff?

"Of course not" Beth laughed. "Your horse needs very little. All this stuff is for you. As a horse-owner, it's in your contract to collect as much totally unnecessary tack and equipment as you can. How else are saddlers and manufacturers of equine clothing and gear going to retire to the Bahamas?"

"But..." I tried "but?"

"Honest!" Beth couldn't stop laughing.

Mum and Jen drifted, a trifle blearily, across to inspect our handiwork.

"Wow! Rubber matting!" Jen said "really state of the Art!"

"What's all this stuff for?" Mum was staring at what could be a tack auction laid out on the concrete.

"It's what every horse owner needs, apparently" I told her.

"You need all these whips? How kinky is that!" Mum nudged Jen.

"This is a small part of it" Beth said seriously "this doesn't include all the riding wear you need. At least four pairs of jods, long boots, jodhpur boots, half-chaps, wellies, water-proof coat, hacking jacket, showing jacket, gilet…"

"STOP!" Mum shouted "I'm rapidly going off the idea of keeping this pony!"

"Then of course…" Beth was enjoying herself "hacking out is fine, but you might want to compete… in which case…"

"Don't tell me!" Mum hollered "A trailer?"

"Well… you're getting the idea… but nowadays there are so many restrictions on what size of car you can tow with that… sorry!… you'll need a big powerful Range Rover to tow with… or… buy a horsebox!"

"I don't want to hear this" Mum covered her ears with her hands.

Struggling to redeem the situation – even though I knew it was only half-serious – I said "I'll be happy to hack out. Nothing else. I've got all I need here"

"Except feed, hay, a live-in blacksmith, a boyfriend who's a vet, and an uncle who could offer you a cheap deal on insurance" Jen muttered blackly.

"Aaaargh!" my mother squealed "I need a drink!"

Already a little wobbly, they staggered off, arm in arm, towards the Midget-shack in search of another bottle.

"Mum doesn't normally drink" I told Beth conversationally.

"Obviously making up for lost time then" she commented drily. "Hey… I don't care… she's great fun. And anyway, better to dump all this info about what having a horse costs on her when she's a bit… er… sheets and wind spring to mind…"

"So what will I need?" I could ask now that Mum was out of ear-shot.

"Oh… all this… and lots more…"

"You are kidding?"

"Er… er… .No!"

***

Sitting in the dust bowl that we imaginatively call our garden, we sipped tea and ate beetroot sandwiches. I did say beetroot, not cucumber; and yes, I DO know the difference. When the cupboard is bare, my mother becomes creative. At least there was yummy carrot cake for seconds.

Mid May; the sun had suddenly found its power. The woozy siblings, having laughed too much, drunk too much and probably eaten too much, fell into an ungainly sleep with their mouths open and their fillings revealed.

"They're great" Beth assured me as she caught my disgusted glance. "And now I must go"

"Oh" me, disappointed.

"I've had a fantastic time" she said swiping her finger round the plate. "I can't tell you what it's like to be the expert for once"

"What d'you mean?"

"Imagine, o pea brain, what it's like to be the youngest in a house full of brilliant people who run a hugely successful feed supplies business and a very popular livery yard… my sister is a teacher to the stars and writes articles in horse magazines… my brother is a whizz junior show-jumper. How d'you think I feel?"

"Oh, Beth… I had no idea" I felt really guilty and mean. I'd dumped all my problems on her, gone on endlessly about her fantastic family… and imagined that she was the luckiest girl alive.

"Well… common mistake" she laughed ruefully. "but why d'you think I don't compete at the level of the rest of them? Why I do Working Hunter one week, Dressage another, Trec, Games… It's because I don't want to specialise… I want to have fun… but mainly because I know I can't ever be brilliant at anything"

"I bet you could" I said stoutly.

"Huh! They'd be in my face! They would know best! They'd have my soul for breakfast…" she shouted, then dropped her voice as Mum snorted in her sleep. "Now you know. And today was great… I'll come back and help you sort all that stuff out of the tack room."

"I need you to: I haven't a clue what most of it's for" I laughed.

"All the feed in the bins… throw it away… it will be mouldy by now and probably give him colic"

"What's colic?"

"AAARGH!" she squealed "You definitely DO need help"

"I thought it was a baby thing" I said, scuffing my trainer on the gravel.

"There, there" she soothed sarcastically "Aunty Beth will sort you out"

"You going?" Mum mumbled, doing a fair impression of Patsy from Absolutely Fabulous.

"Yes… thanks for the… er… afternoon tea" Beth said politely, giving me a grin.

"I wanted a ride" Jen slurred, shaking her head and rubbing her eyes.

"There's probably a law against being in charge of a horse while under the influence…" Mum scowled at her.

"Do you really want a ride?" Beth didn't know whether to be rude or polite.

"Relive my childhood and all that" Jen told her.

"Come on then" Beth said, ignoring me rolling my eyes at her.

"Me too. I wanna ride, too" Mum leapt to her feet.

"If we lead them up the lane, you can ride Teddy back

home and leave them to walk off their... um... alcohol" Beth whispered as we tacked up the ponies.

"Hats" she told the women.

"Hats. Hats" they twittered, in turn, trying on mine, then Beth's, then one we'd found in the tack room stuffed with shredded bits of paper and fabric threads; we didn't tell them it had been a nest to a family of mice. Mum drew the short straw – I hoped the mice wouldn't see her and scream for the mice-police that their home was being abducted.

Fortunately, the ladies took the riding very seriously and stopped parping around. In the dappled light beneath the trees, it was cool. The ponies walked along with a rhythmic clip clop on tarmac. I held Teddy's bridle; Beth led Zeb and they behaved beautifully.

As we hauled the women off our ponies and mounted ourselves, I had a shock. Teddy made it quite clear that he wanted to go with his new mate. Inexperienced, I had so far never had a problem with him. HELP!

"Keep your reins short, squeeze with your legs, and don't let him turn. Go Now" Teddy tried to whizz round to follow Zeb; my mother was wittering about leading me, but Beth said "No. You can do this. It's Make or Break Time, Sara. Go for it"

And I did. And Teddy stopped dancing and prancing and we clattered home like a coach-and-four with lots of noise and hallooing from the two daft women following behind. There's more to this riding lark than I thought!

Chapter 13

Lying on my mattress I smiled into the darkness, remembering all the laughter. With the window open to disperse the strong scent of fresh emulsion, I could feel a warm breeze on my face.

Beneath my window, Mum and Jen were still sitting on the picnic chairs, talking. The mumble of conversation was soothing; sleepy night-time birds made small musical noises. I tried to identify them, but I'm still a townie.

This is a quiet corner of the world. Depending on wind direction, sometimes we can hear a faint hum of noise from a motorway. From the other direction we hear traffic noise from the main road that runs through the village at the top of 'our' lane. Ned the Farmer occasionally wakens us at an ungodly hour driving past on his green tractor to feed stock in one of the fields beyond our house. Other times, we hear the slow progress of his black and white dairy herd shuffling towards the milking parlour and a fat feed while machines drain their milk. Far cry from the dairy maid sitting on a three-legged stool with her forehead pressed against Daisy's side while her work-rough hands squeezed milk from swollen udder into shiny metal bucket.

Ooh ar, m'dear! I'm really taking to the country life. I can converse knowledgeably about the price of... er... barley. Well, maybe not! but I'm getting there.

It's not at all what I expected. I'd imagined mud and wellies, cowpats on all the roads and streets, broad accents saying stuff like 'we just comed up from Zomerzet where the zider apples grow' (a favourite song of my Gran, who lives not in Somerset but in Spain). I thought there'd be bulls everywhere but apparently all that one-to-one hanky-panky between cow and bull (or mare and stallion for that matter) is a thing of the past as Artificial Insemination rules. And far from wandering around in smocks, carrying pitch-forks and chewing stems of straw, some farmers are, of necessity, so computer literate nowadays that they put most of us to shame.

So there I was, lying contentedly on my (thin!) mattress beneath the window where I could watch the stars, thinking of night-birds and my pony dreaming in his field, and my mum, aunt and friend with tears of laughter rolling down their faces. I couldn't recall ever feeling so contented.

Befuddled, I half woke from a dream. Breeze on my face felt cool now, and the birds had long gone to roost in branch or nest. Listening, I shook myself awake. I had drifted off into sleep to the hypnotic murmur of voices under my window, accompanied by the clinking of glasses, the odd louder "Ouch! I'm being eaten alive by bloody midges!" or half-stifled giggles.

Sitting up, I strained to hear. The only sound was sobbing.

Padding barefoot on the cold floor-boards, I peered through the window. In the gloom, I could make out two shapes. Gradually, my eyes adjusted to the dimness. My aunt had pulled her chair closer to Mum's; her hand was stretched across the gap, holding Mum's hand. Head bent so low it was almost touching her knees, Mum was weeping uncontrollably.

My first instinct was to rush downstairs to find out what could be so bad that my mum's heart was breaking. Second thoughts told me to wait.

"Let it all out…" Jen's voice was soothing.

Mum wailed louder; this was serious; normally she would be considerate about waking me.

"I still love him" she blubbered.

"I know… I know…" Jen's gentle voice.

"How could he…?" more sobbing.

"You've been so brave… held it all together for Sara… gone through so much…" Well, yes, her voice was rather slurred; maybe this was partly down to a surfeit of booze… but… it felt very serious. I pressed my face against the cold frame, peering for a better view.

"I have, haven't I?" Mum whimpered "And sometimes I didn't want to… I wanted somebody to look after ME…" her voice rose in a plaintive wail. "There were days when I felt I'd got rigor mortis; I'd smiled so much my face was stuck like that…" she giggled and Jen sniffed and upended the empty wine bottle. "When she said he'd been waiting outside school…" hiccup "I was so JEALOUS… I couldn't even go and pick her up… so JEALOUS that he wanted her… not me"

"He's a bum" Jen murmured "You don't wanna go back to him… no good…"

"I KNOW that" Mum moaned "but I still LOVE him, don't I?" angrily.

Then she started crying again and it sounded like the deepest pain I'd ever heard. And tears dripped onto my window-sill from my helpless eyes.

Wide-eyed and shivering, I lay flat on my mattress, hot-wired with shock.

How? Why? What?

She still loved him? Really? But Why?

How could she? How could I? No answer to that.

All these months... I thought she was angry with him.

I was angry. Anger made me close up against him. But he's my Father.

A small mournful voice in my head said "He was her Husband"

All these months I had made it out to be all about ME.

That was all I thought about; My pain, my hurt, my betrayal.

While my mother was protecting me, hiding her feelings to spare mine I had never considered that she was hurting far more than me.

Covering my face with shaking hands, realisation flooded through me.

I'd made it all about me and in reality it was nothing to do with me.

He hadn't left me – he'd left her. I wasn't even that important in his life.

This was stuff between adults; I was only a satellite to my mother's planet.

Not childish, but absolutely infantile.

Me Me Me

And instead of slapping me down, my grieving mother had comforted me, and spared me, and been patient with me, and taken all the knocks on my behalf.

I was hot with a shame so intense that it caused a flood of self-loathing to drip boiling tears down my face.

In the city where I used to live, it's never quiet, not even at night. There is always a hum of traffic; a hint of sirens, reminding everybody that the course of lives has suddenly changed. An arrest; a smashing of metal against metal and a life snuffs out; a fire destroying a family home. Some of the time, you learn to block it out with selective hearing.

There's always light, too. A yellow street-light haze hangs over every road and street and garden. It's never dark, except in those scary back-alley moments when you don't want it to be.

Petrol fumes hang in the air; you get so used to it, you don't notice. Birds start the day with a good coughing session. In the dead of night some drunken idiots on their way home just HAVE to test the echo in the street. It's impressive, you can hear it four streets away, and it unsettles slumbering dogs.

Shivering on my mattress, I listened to the scurrying of small creatures in dried grasses and dead leaves, and waited for my relatives to shut the hell up and go to bed. I could hardly bear to think of my mother. At first I tried to tell myself she hadn't meant all that stuff… it was unaccustomed booze talking. But I've played baby long enough; time to face the truth.

When I heard them bumping around inside the house, flushing the loo, and turning taps on and off, I crawled across the floor and dragged a track suit on over my pyjamas. I needed to be outside – away from them. Pulling on socks and trainers, I carefully eased open my bedroom door. There's a huge disadvantage in being two floors up – its two staircases down and I haven't had time to work out which steps creak yet. One of them was running a tap, loud in the quiet. In my mother's unfinished bedroom, the other one was banging about, organising sleeping bags maybe.

Like a cat burglar, I eased myself down one stair at a time, softly to avoid noise; then along the corridor past the bathroom, and down the stairs to the ground floor, less careful now that my movements were disguised by the sound of running water.

I crept out of the back door. There was a lingering scent

of citronella from the lemony candles they'd lit to deter insects. I picked my way carefully between picnic chairs and table, skirting round a discarded toilet gleaming white and surreal in the heavy darkness, and then to the gate.

Peering through the gloom, I squinted at every shadow and dark patch of hedge, seeking Teddy. No sign of him in the lighter part of the field, so I slipped through the gate, careful with the catch, and blinked my way along the hedge.

Meditating, maybe; more likely dozing, my pony jumped in surprise when I bumped into him. I was pretty startled myself. At least he didn't flick up his heels and zoom off into the distance. I smiled at the lovely wuffling greeting he gave me. Reaching out my hand, it was almost like being magnetized towards him.

Touch is so wonderful!

Why do we use it so little?

I can't remember last time I felt another human being. My mother would hug me if I didn't shudder with horror and back off. If I should allow her to hold me, I wouldn't dream of hugging her back – of feeling the texture of her skin, the pulse of her body.

A mother with a baby... yeah! They do all that stroking and petting stuff.

What a sad state that... after that... hey, you want touch, you pay a therapist; hey, you want to stroke – get a dog!

What happens?

Oh I guess at some point it comes back in the form of lovey-dovey stuff between consenting adults. It's no wonder people can't wait to hook up... they've been missing out on a seriously powerful form of communication for... what ten... fifteen years?

Out there in the middle of the night, surrounded by a soft silence and shrouded by darkness, I allowed my hands to rest on my horse and it was pure magic. It felt as though every pulse of blood, every rhythmical beat of his heart, the movements of his gut, the quivering of his breathing… were all being offered to me; like a gift.

Briefly I wondered how he 'feels' me. I leaned against his neck, face close to his, so that he could sense me through his skin. If that's the way it works!

Smells, maybe? His nostrils appear to twitch a lot and he breathes on my hands and face as though registering their smell.

What did Jen say? Oh yes! Something about horses feeling our auras, Hmm. Yup, that's the sort of thing Jen would say. And maybe she's right!

With a soft whoosh of feathers, a blunt headed shape glided silently across my vision. Straining to follow its flight in the velvet darkness, I heard a cooing Whooo. An owl; I smiled. Am I losing the plot? Me, standing in a field in the early hours of the morning, stroking a horse and smiling because I've spotted an owl. Bring on the White Coats!

Teddy moved, bumping my face. "I've been really awful" I told him "I'm so ashamed" What I love about this pony is, he has no sense of social conventions. For an answer, he walked forward, head down, looking for grass. I moved with him. "I can see you don't care" I told him, resting my arm across the top of his back "but I have to say this: I've been so SO selfish…" his skin twitched beneath my arm "I never thought about anyone else. It was all about me…" His coat felt like velvet. "d'you know what I mean…? I only thought about him leaving ME… my poor mum, who loved – actually still does love – him, is gutted. He was her love, her husband, her rock, her future, her security… Now he's gone… well… she's got to look after me, earn a living… sleep in an empty bed… face a future without him…"

We moved slowly across the field, my pony and I, seeking out succulent blades of grass; his tail swishing away late-night midges. I felt every move he made and was comforted.

"And as well as dealing with all that, and trying to make a house into a home… she had me to deal with! I've been so brattish… I've thrown tantrums, sworn at her, been rebellious, rude, disgraced her in public…"

Teddy chomped contentedly. I noticed the distant sky was showing a paler shade of dark in the east. It didn't seem important that I'd had no sleep; the communication with another living being was of much more significance. That, and the fact that I had to stay wide awake to avoid getting my toes crushed by my best friend.

There's something magical about talking to a horse. You know when you have a really good friend – somebody you really like – but they annoy the hell out of you by jumping in and supplying the last word of your every sentence? It's hateful because you know they're hovering like vultures to grab the juicy bits of the conversation. Pretending to listen to you, they're drooling, waiting for their turn… and there they go! Yeah! Grab that last word and it lets them in.

So instead of chatting happily, you spend a tense time being extremely energetic with sentence construction so that at that last moment when… you've nearly said it… and you see a red mouth open ready to snatch the end of your sentence… yehaaa… with unrivalled agility, you change the ending so they are left with mouth hanging open and slaver dribbling down their chin.

Okay, a slight exaggeration maybe!

Horses don't do that!

They stand quietly and let you rant and rave with no desire to steal your ideas or second-guess you. Very restful it is, too. You hear your voice saying rubbishy things and edit as you go. Whiney tone of voice? Only the horse hears it; vow never to do it again.

My pony is a mirror. An echo. I hear my voice bounce back at me. Head low, he seeks out tasty green shoots. All this talking palaver, he seems to say, why bother?

Blackbirds are doing vocal exercises in hedge-bottoms; a thrush practises scales from the topmost branch of a birch tree. At the margin of the world, the sky is tinted a rosy hue. Somewhere over the edge a great golden sun is waiting to push upwards and startle the earth into waking.

Fetching the bridle, I persuade my pony to raise his head and come with me – out into the lanes, between the sleeping trees, to taste dew upon our tongues, and let the wind into our faces.

Delay the unfurling of the day; I have so much to face. My poor mother, having a brat like me… can I grow up soon enough to earn forgiveness?

This is the first day of a new life. Woopidooo! Shall I bother? Or Not?

***

Fell asleep in maths. Who doesn't?

Unfortunately I got caught. The arm my head was resting on slipped, throwing me, with total lack of dignity off my chair. No damage done, except to my street credibility.

I laughed so much I had to pretend I was crying. Not 'off with her head' but 'off to Mrs Hughes' for some superficial idea of counselling. Woop-woo! Played the Joker and was let off with a warning, a concerned hand on my shoulder and a low urgent plea to "Come and talk to me if you need to"

Wait! Yup… here it comes…"My door is always open"

Close to disgrace in the giggles department again, but managed to nod my head gravely and mumble a thank you before pushing a tissue over my eyes and scooting off to the loos.

Surprise, Surprise!

My arrival home was greeted by Aunty Jen grabbing my hand and rushing me upstairs. Part of the surprise was that Jen is still here when she was supposed to go home by train this morning.

Second part of the surprise was that instead of our feet hammering and echoing on wooden boards... wow! soft carpets!

My attic rooms have both been carpeted with a soft creamy colour, almost the same shade as the walls. I wasn't sure about this but Cyclops-Jen with 'the good eye' assured me it would work, especially with the varnished woodwork. Cream walls, cream floor... I'm not sure that I'll know which way up I am. But... it does work. When all my soft furnishings are installed, it will be fantastic.

Stuff homework! I persuaded Jen to help me furnish Mum's room, smelling of new carpet, all wonderful pale lavender colours.

Rushing to be done before she came home, we tugged and hauled her bed up the stairs, and together we (as Jen put it) 'dressed the bed' with the lovely silky duvet and cushions, and the new curtains she'd had made. In contrast to the mauve carpet, we found a soft white furry rug to lay beside the bed.

Only then did I allow myself to go and ride Teddy, while Jen magically knocked up a meal in what is almost a kitchen.

"Why is Jen still here?" I asked Mum after she had childishly rolled on the new carpet, squidged her toes into the luxurious white rug and bounced on the bed.

"She stayed to deal with the carpet fitter" Mum said vaguely, closing the curtains, then re-opening them; because she could!

"So is she going home tomorrow?"

"Ask her yourself, Sara"

"She's avoiding the subject"

"Hmmmm…"

"What is going on, Mum?"

Maybe it was the use of the word 'Mum' when normally I grunt at her! "Oh… I think she and Dom are having a few problems"

"No! They love each other!"

Mum looked straight into my eyes, very serious. "People do love each other and still have problems" she said gently.

"Are they going to…? Has he…? Is there somebody else?" I asked, scandalised.

"No… they need some time apart… that's all… Now… shall we get your bed in, then you can start sleeping like a civilised person too"

"You're changing the subject" I accused.

"Maybe, but it isn't my business to discuss with anybody else"

"I'm not anybody else" I said indignantly "I'm related to her… and I love her… and I care…"

omygod! I used the L word! My mother jolted like she'd been prodded!

"Maybe Jen will tell you when she's ready" Mum said gently.

Despite their matching bloodshot eyes from the previous evening's binge drinking, they were in good humour as we wrestled my divan-base up the staircase to my attic; then the mattress; then dragged the old mattress I'd been sleeping on down the stairs and hauled it into a skip.

Then, unfortunately, I had to do my homework as they settled down in the lounge on the manky picnic chairs because it had started to rain; and out came a new bottle of wine. I couldn't help wondering if they were celebrating

… or drowning their sorrows.

Chapter 14

Next morning as I waited at the top of the lane for Maggie and Beth to pick me up, I noticed three heads in the car as it drove towards me.

As I climbed in, I realised Leo was sitting in the front passenger seat. His blond shaggy hair was longer than when I'd last seen him, and he'd acquired a tan in the lovely warm weather we'd been having. He looked more than ever like a beach bum.

I Hate

I Really Hate

Blushing.

Grunts all round; Leo flashed me a dazzling smile and I sort-of grimaced in return. As I flopped down next to Beth in the back, trying to stash my school bags out of the way, she prodded my knee with her finger and said in a very low voice "Do. Not. Go. There"

"Eurrrr?????"

"You know! Don't Even Think It!"

"Don't know what you're talking about" I hissed back.

Now, in case you're sitting back with a smug expression on your face, dear reader, thinking "Aha! So Leo the beach bum show-jumper is to be the Love-Interest" let me discombobulate (love that word!) you.

And... if you are now thinking "Ah, well... if not Leo... it must be Wayne Shane Duane... Forget It!

If Wayne Shane Duane was the last man swinging from a branch, scratching his armpits and spitting fruit pips at me in a world where all other men had long vanished... I would still choose being slapped about the head with two dead fish.

Wayne and I have come to an unspoken agreement. I will make him cups of tea... but not in the nude. I may be a girl (all he's interested in) but I'm not up for grabs.

***

WEYHAY!

Moving day!

Not!

At least most people moving house have the dignity of a van transporting their bags and chattels. No such elegance for us. We became a raiding party, rummaging about in the well-stuffed garage shouting "catch this..." "do we need this..." "grab the other end of this, will you..." With the finesse of a troupe of dancing baboons, we dragged furniture and boxes, and enough black plastic bin-bags to fill a land-fill site, out onto the drive.

"Let's get Shane here... he'd enjoy doing this" Mum said.

"Wayne..." I corrected.

"Hmm... him as well..." Mum murmured absent-mindedly, ripping the corner of a black bag to see what it contained.

"You do it" I told Jen "I don't want him to think it was my suggestion"

"Not your type?"

"My type would realise I have eyes and that my brain isn't centred in my boobs" I sniped.

The amateur removal team who'd lovingly stashed all our

worldly possessions, and thus, my inheritance, in the garage, had obviously been a couple of girlies. Mum and Jen, actually. The job hadn't exactly been done systematically or logically. Mainly, bags had been chucked – as high and as far as possible towards the back of the garage. Every item of furniture was therefore clamped down under the weight of precariously balanced bags.

Fortunately, before we girlies did each other lasting harm, the rickety Lurv-Bus arrived bearing Wayne and Joe. Testosterone fuelled and eager to demonstrate muscle, they barged in and ventured forth where we had only teetered, giggling.

So – at last – Moving Day.

Not only was I to sleep like a princess tonight but the small third bedroom, which had been earmarked by Mum as her study-cum-office, would be Jen's squat, for the time being.

Our kitchen was obviously being fitted by elves who crept in and worked very hard, when I was at school. I never even learned the fitter's name, except 'you know, the guy who's fitting the kitchen…' Anyway, he has been persuaded to assemble a load of crappy flat-pack furniture, rather than risk it being in 'lovingly hand-crafted by Girlies' unmistakable style. Mum and Jen had boasted they would do it themselves, but after a wasted evening trying to understand the instructions for a book-case, they decided obscene amounts of money shoved in the direction of the chief elf – would give them a better quality of life (and more time for alcohol abuse).

He is therefore going to magic a range of wardrobes in my bedroom, and a computer work-station so that I can start handing in homework that is at least legible. Mum is having a range of fitted wardrobes in her room and a computer desk in the third bedroom, i.e. Jens. All this will appear by osmosis when we are out of the house. Though, I'm not sure where Jen is when all this happens... maybe she chats him up... or helps...?

This is SO exciting! I shall have a choice of clothes. My books will be unpacked. Boxes and boxes full of meaningful hieroglyphics will be tenderly placed in my room ready for translation and sorting, and then, no doubt, a trip to the paper bank at the recycling plant.

Soon we shall live like proper civilised people – sleeping on beds, sitting in chairs, and actually eating meals prepared in our own kitchen instead of the steamy aromatic back-room of the Chinese Takeaway. Will we adapt? Will we remember how it's all done? Will my mother learn how to make toast without adding to the earth's carbon emissions?

Joe and Wayne are as excited as we are, and forget to be Cool as giggling affects us all. This could be something to do with the bottle of wine my mother and aunt have uncorked – and which appears to be going down faster than they are drinking. Hmmm... maybe our two yoofs are helping themselves to a quick swig when nobody's looking. If I hadn't totally brain-washed myself into the 'my body is a temple' philosophy, I'd secretly quite like to take a crafty swig myself. Just to see what it's all about, you understand; all in the inter-est of scientific research... Heaven forbid that I should want to become silly and giggly like them...

For years I have toned and strained my body; I've worn, not only the proverbial hair-shirt, but hair knickers and socks as well. I'm now trying hard to recall why denying myself any fun, creature-comforts or luxuries was essential to the rising of my star. Did it really make me tougher or did I enjoy being a martyr?

Deprivation is a thing of the past, I'd told my aunt as we hit the shops with purses full of plastic. The plastic, of course, was hers, but Mum had sanctioned the spending of obscene amounts of dosh providing it would stop me behaving like a brat.

The exotic fruits of our retail therapy were in evidence now as we lovingly drew out our haul. Gorgeous Indian fabrics in scarlet and damask; silks and satins beaded with intricate designs. Jen, teetering on a broken blue milk crate at full stretch to hang my curtains... splendour untold! My aunt the Cyclops really has An Eye; she'd said "trust me: I once watched a make-over programme on telly...". I had trusted. She bought maroon and carmine and ruby fabrics to make flimsy curtains. "Layering is In" she said adding voile in palest rose and filmy white, juggling them, between the reds. At some point, she's managed to sew them into a fan; they looked sumptuous at my windows.

Secretly I couldn't help wondering whether this was really 'me'. As I lovingly shook out the silky bedspread with its detailed tiny patterns in minute vermilion beads and fragments of mirror, I tried to imagine myself in dirty jods and mud covered boots, flinging myself down on it. A bit of a clash of images there!

We'd chosen plump cushions decorated with tiny flowers, glass and ornate patterns. The colours clashed – too many reds – too many shades. Against the bland clotted cream walls and carpet it looked fantastic. Little beaded cherry and magenta bedside lights threw a florid tint onto the walls.

"Cor!" said Wayne, peeping in through the door.

"Crumbs! A Madam's boudoir!" laughed my mother.

"I'd like to sleep in it" commented Joe, then blushed as scarlet as the furry bedside rug. "I didn't mean..." he stuttered when we all laughed.

"In your dreams" I muttered out of the side of my mouth.

***

A few days later, I was sitting on the back door-step, prising mud out of the treads of my trainers when Wayne eased past me on his way outside for a 'Smoko'. Blowing smoke out of the side of his mouth, he asked conversationally "D'ya want to er like er go out sometime like?"

Surprised I asked "With you?"

"Yeah"

"Er… no… it's alright thanks" a bizarre thing to say, but I was wrong-footed.

I poked at the dried mud, my hand squashed inside the trainer and asked "Why?"

"Dunno… thought you might be lusting after my bod or something"

Emphatically I assured him "No… not at all… but thanks for asking"

"S'a'right" cheerfully. He could at least pretend to be disappointed.

Drawing deep breath on his cigarette, he blew air through his nostrils and watched it vanish. "Joe wouldn't mind, either" he observed.

More weird by the minute! "Wouldn't mind what?" I asked.

"Y'know… like… taking you out…"

Should I be flattered? I'M NOT!

"Don't think I'd really be interested in joining a long queue of girls to sample the Lurv-bus."

"You'd be the first" Wayne grinned at me.

"What d'you mean?"

"Isn't and never has been a Lurv-Machine" Wayne said "he's got a vivid imagination has Joe…"

"Interesting" I said, pushing a hand into each trainer and banging them together to dislodge the last pellets of dried mud "but I'm still not likely to go out with him"

"S'a'right" Wayne said casually "don't suppose he's that

bothered… it was just like er… if you wanted to give it a try…"

Formally, I bowed my head as though acknowledging a compliment and said "Well… thank you both for your offers… you certainly know how to make a girl feel special" (NOT!!!)

Smug-face threw down his cigarette butt and stomped his Doc Marten steel capped toe on it. "Well… if you change your mind…" he pushed past me and I could hear him humming a discordant tune as he went back to magnolia emulsion.

I won't!

***

Sorting out the Tack Room is taking FOREVER. There is so much stuff, and I haven't a clue what most of it's for. Among all the bits of paper and show schedules and vaccination certificates for Teddy, there were some books. Now, instead of relying on Beth to give me endless mini-lectures, I'm identifying each object, whether brush, boots, rugs or tools, in the books and learning what it's for. Imagine that – it all takes a very long time. Still, I'm learning! I now know that white horses are referred to as grey and black horses are very rarely truly black. Front legs are called forelegs, back legs are hindlegs. Horses don't run – they trot, canter or gallop (or, if trained that way, do a lope, unless they are Icelandic ponies in which case they have two extra gaits, the tölt and the flying pace).

Okay, sounds lame; I've learned lots of other things, too.

Busy with my tidying and cataloguing, I grumbled to myself when I heard a car stopping outside the front of our house. Nosiness prevailed as we don't get many visitors apart from workmen in plaster – or paint-splattered overalls and I wandered towards the house.

Mum and Jen were in the kitchen desecrating veggies for tea. But it was Jen's tomato-red face which drew my attention as I pushed open the back door. She looked like she'd had her head stuck in the oven. Her face was pink with perspiration, her eyes red, rolling and popping and it seemed even her hair stood on end in an unattractive frizz.

The reason was obvious. Nervously jangling his car keys in his pocket and looking very ill at ease was her husband (I should say ABANDONED husband) Dominic.

I haven't been informed of the situation in their household so had no idea whether his appearance was a Good Thing or a Bad Thing. Jen's eyes continued to pop. Mum frog-marched me out of the kitchen, announcing in a very strong cheerful voice that we need to "sort something out…" So subtle, my parent! I wondered whether Jen needed moral support, but Mum was hauling me away from the house like the Hound of the Baskervilles was after us. No use resisting my mother when she's in that mood!

Teddy's field has been rolled by our affable neighbour Farmer Ned; the hawthorn hedges have been sliced down to a minimum by his powerful tractor-thingey with cutters attached. Grass has grown. And grown.

Despite a surfeit of grass, Teddy is always delighted to have visitors and rushes to the gate to greet each one individually and effusively. 'Holding Court' my mother calls it.

"You'll have to watch his weight" she remarked, scratching his neck with her fingernails.

"Apart from the parts of the field where the old droppings were really deep, there's loads of grass" I had my hand over my eyes against the bright evening sun.

"We'll have to ask Angie what to do about it; we may have to buy an electric fence to restrict his grazing" Mum was talking to me, but her eyes kept slithering back to the house.

She can be SO NOSEY!

"What d'you think's happening?" I asked slyly.

"Don't know… I just hope…"

"What? What does Jen want?" I HATE being a teenager; adults always stop short… you know, they start to tell you something then stop because it's rude or adult or porno-graphic or… whatever!

"Hmmmm… hard to say…" *See what I mean!*

"Does she love him?"

"Oh, Sara…" she sighed "love isn't always the answer"

"Why not? It should be. If two people love each other…"

"You and your father loved each other" for a moment, she looked directly into my eyes "but that wasn't enough, was it…?" then turned away.

"I wasn't married to him" I protested.

"Exactly. He had never promised to be faithful to you. He still loves you. But… you're hurt… you won't give him a second chance, will you?" turning, she started to walk slowly back towards the house.

"Mum!"

"It's all so complicated. Love is never simple" she reached out and touched my arm – a rough little rub with her fingertips.

"Think I'll stick to horses" I muttered gloomily.

I heard her sad little laugh. What is it with adults?

I'm beginning to have a horrible feeling that they really don't know all that much. Maybe they don't know any more than kids do. I imagined it was in the Parents' Charter that they had to know EVERYTHING. At least… well, about lurv and all that stuff.

It seems to do nothing but make them unhappy. Before I become depressed and sad, I shall have to go on the Internet to find some answers.

Or not!

"Oh!" my mother's voice was flat and disappointed. Peering round her, I felt the same: the kitchen was deserted. The new granite work-surface was littered with vegetable peelings and tops and tails. A lonely carrot awaited the boiling pot. No steam – Jen had abandoned her post, and her culinary duties.

"Looks like we're cooking then" I nudged my mother forward.

"Shall we make enough for Dom as well...?" she mused.

I stuck my head round the lounge door; not yet finished... didn't imagine they'd be there... but at least I could see both their cars were still parked out in the lane. "They'll be back" I assured her "must have gone off for a walk to avoid you eavesdropping"

"Sara! As if!"

Long after we'd eaten and cleared away, they returned, hand in hand. Ah!

Jen looked as though a light had been ignited inside her; she was absolutely radiant. Stuffy old Dom wore a very smug expression.

"You two alright, then...?" Mum asked.

"Yeah!" came the enthusiastic response from both of them.

"but... I think we might go now..." Jen said hesitantly.

"Oh!" Mum was deflated. If they scarpered now, she wouldn't find out the gossip. "er won't you have something to eat first... you must be starving"

Blushing, they exchanged glances, fingers intertwined.

"Not very hungry..." Dom glanced at Jen, smiling "maybe we'll hit the road and stop off for a pub meal if we feel... er... hungry"

"Soz" Jen mouthed at Mum "but we need to go... I'll go

and pack my things…"

"I'll come and help" Mum jumped in eagerly, determined to learn the terms of this reconciliation. *She Won't Give Up, Will She!*

"All's well and all that…" she sighed, slipping her arm round my shoulder as we stood in the lane waving goodbye to the happy couple.

"Is it?" I asked.

"For now" she squeezed me "there are no guarantees about anything, Sara"

"I wish there were. I hate changes" I said.

"That's what life is; you gotta ride with it, kid"

"Have you? All the stuff with Dad and divorce and everything…? I asked.

"Mmm… aaaah… well…" she laughed. "I will… eventually…"

Chapter 15

The invitation to a meeting at Oak Tree had sounded very formal, and I was quite nervous. Why, I asked Mum, would they invite me to a business meeting... or any other kind of meeting for that matter? "Hmmm" her usual evasive reply!

When I arrived, the meeting had obviously been going on for a long time. The huge kitchen table was littered with dirty coffee cups, bits of paper, broken pencils, files and invoices. All the family members sagged in exhaustion.

"Oh come in, Sara..." Mrs Southward called, seeing me sidling nervously through the door. She patted the only empty chair and I slithered into it, grimacing at everybody.

Heeelllpppp!

Beth went to fetch my favourite tipple – Ribena and lemonade – and I slid down in my seat, trying to be as invisible as possible as Predictions and Accounts and Profiles and Business Plans were finalised.

OUCH! HELP! What am I doing here?

When all the grown-up talk seemed to be finishing, and papers and files were pushed into brief-cases, the atmosphere lightened. "Sorry about that" Maggie said. "It always takes longer than we anticipate."

"'s'a'right" I muttered, wishing that Beth would sit next to me (even hold my hand!).

After all the heavy stuff, and me feeling like a pork-pie at a vegetarian Christmas Party, what came next was even heavier! Be afraid. Be VERY afraid! I wanted my mum!

I was being Head-Hunted! Well… offered a Saturday job! ME!!!

Weyhey!

I was just starting to understand that Angie and Maggie were talking to me – as in, offering me a job, when Beth threw a Wobbly, pushed back her chair so violently that it fell over, and dashed out of the kitchen making wailing banshee noises. Shocked silence.

At length Angie addressed the air with "What did I say?"

Mrs Southward, Maggie and I all shook our heads, looking puzzled.

"I'll go and find her" Mrs Southward said.

"No… give her a few minutes" Angie suggested "then Sara can go…"

Thanks!

"Probably PMT" Maggie mumbled, knocking the edges of a sheaf of papers to form a neat pile.

"I'll put the kettle on" said Mrs Southward. *Typical mother!*

Eventually I was dispatched in search of Beth. I knew where to look; exactly where I would have been when needing a good blubber – draped over a pony!

Her face was red and mottled, eyes bloodshot and she was still snivelling into a shredded wad of Kleenex. I stood at the stable door and cleared my throat. Her smile was like a watery sun after a storm.

"Listen…" I said, wanting to get in first "if you hate the idea so much, I'll say no to the job…"

"What!?"

"I'll say no. I certainly don't want to steal your job or anything…"

Blowing her nose was a snotty business; I delved in my pockets and found her another tissue. "Steal my job? What're you talking about?"

"Well… I don't know. Really. But why else would you be… er… blubb… er crying?"

"You're not stealing my job, you dork" Beth smeared her hand over her face.

"Well… why…?"

"Didn't you hear what they said? Weren't you listening?" she cried indignantly. A horrible feeling that maybe I'd misunderstood, washed over me. Perhaps they weren't offering me a job; ouch – I'd really made a fool of myself, then…

"What… then…?" I stuttered.

"They said…" Beth took a huge shuddering breath "that I'm important in all this business… that I do a good job…"

"Yeah? So?"

Hhhheeeelllpppp… what's going down, here?

"I always thought…" Beth gulped hard as she explained "that I was rubbish… I wasn't a junior show jumper like Leo, or a brilliant rider like Angie and Maggie and Mum… I would never make a teacher like them because I've no patience with people… and I'm not very competitive so I would never be an eventer… and I think showing classes are a bit Naff… but they said - ALL of them – how brilliant I am with young horses. I heard them. They said I'm terrific and bring them on in just the right way… and you are to help me…

I always felt such a failure…" Beth was laughing and crying all at the same time. Zeb turned his head and gave her a funny look.

"Oh Come On!" I shouted "they've just made you Head of Department!"

Together, draped over Zeb's warm back, we collapsed into hysterical laughter. That was how Angie found us.

"Everything alright, then?" she asked.

"It's fine" I answered for Beth. "I think maybe your sister has needed a bit more praise for work well done…" I pulled a funny face to Angie behind Beth's back "and it came as a shock to know you think so highly of her…"

"Oh Beth!" Angie rushed in and hugged her. "I'm so sorry. We're all so bloody big-headed round here, all so sure of how good we are… it never occurred to us that you felt left out… that you didn't see yourself as having any role in the business…"

"The Empire, you mean…" Beth scoffed.

"Mmmmm… well…" Angie grinned.

"If it's true confession time…" I interrupted "can I say something…?"

"Oh no! Not more Teenage Angst" Angie laughed.

"It's… just… well… I want to enjoy all this horse stuff. I've spent so many years grinding at Gymnastics… without realising that I wasn't enjoying it… I… er… don't want to be sucked back into something like that…"

Zeb wandered over to his haynet, leaving us all standing unsupported in the middle of his stable. "I know" Angie said. "that's why this offer has been made. If you're helping Beth with youngsters and re-schooling, and bringing on the ponies we've backed, then you'll be hacking out together, and showing them traffic, and maybe the odd shows… getting them out and about and used to things…"

"but I'm not good enough…" I protested.

"No, you're not…" Angie said "but you have potential"

"Right…? And…?"

"Oh do shut up, Sahara!" Beth interrupted "You're only angling for compliments"

"Of course I'm not… but I haven't a clue what to do with a 'youngster' – whatever that is" I shouted "and anyway… just because you've been made Head of Department doesn't mean you can tell me to shut up"

Zeb turned his back and deposited a pile of steamy droppings right near Beth's muckers.

"See!" I taunted "that's what Zeb thinks of you"

"What I want…" Angie interrupted "is for you to be here learning stable management. You'll ride different ponies and develop your skills – with a lesson from me each week on something that isn't Teddy. As you progress, you'll work the ponies – Beth will advise – Maggie will advise – I will advise. No way are you ready to be dumped on a green youngster; you wouldn't have a clue! Teddy is an angel"

"and there aren't many of them around" Beth interrupted. All excited now, she shook my arm saying "and you could hack over on Teddy. He could have some company while you're working… and you won't need a lift…"

"It'll be hard work" Angie said "and dirty work… and loads of stuff you hate… it won't be a fun day. But from our point of view, it'll be great for Beth to have someone to help her at shows. It's been rough for you…" she smiled at her sister "cos dad ain't much fun… and often there's been nobody else to go with you. You've never complained… but now. Sara will be there to give you some moral support…"

"and you'll have a clear conscience…" Beth interrupted, nudging Angie.

"Are you SURE about all this?" I pleaded.

"Yup… though it would have been better to have found somebody who doesn't WHINE" Beth laughed.

"Whine? Moi?"

At that moment, Leo strutted past the stable, two huge hay-nets draped over his shoulder. "Wotcha!" he greeted us.

His jodhpurs were really very tight.

I blushed.

"That…" said Angie pointedly, watching Leo's departing bum "of course – could be a distraction"

I blushed more; the colour seemed to be rushing into my face from somewhere in my boots; even my arms were blushing.

"Better not be…" Beth mumbled darkly "I'm not having staff who lust after the stable-lads… and anyway, he'd eat you for breakfast…"

"I'm not…" I protested, but then I remembered a silly conversation between Mum and Jen, and started to giggle helplessly.

Once when Mum came to Oak Tree to pick me up, she'd spotted Leo's blond thatch and described him as 'dishy'.

"Yuk!" I said, concentrating on fastening my seatbelt. She noticed I was blushing and, in the way of viciously cruel relatives, decided to have some fun at my expense.

"I've found you a gorgeous toy boy" she told Jen at tea-time.

"Great" Jen responded without interest "have him yourself. I've got enough problems at the moment"

"He's all muscley and tanned and looks like a surfer boy"

"Really?" Jen perked up.

"No" I shouted rudely "he might LOOK all right but he's a tease… I've seen him with his Groupies"

"He has Groupies?" Jen demanded.

"Fancies himself as a star because he wins jumping classes" I muttered sourly.

"So really he's a cad?" Mum asked.

"a blackguard?" Jen said, though she pronounced it blaggard.

"a bounder…?"

"a low-life…?"

"a Casanova…?"

"No!" I snapped ""He's just a big head." and stomped off, blushing all the way into the roots of my hair.

Remembering this now, I couldn't stop giggling. Beth told me to share it with her or go home; I pulled rude faces and said I'd go home. She might be employing me, I told her, but I hadn't sold my flippin' soul to her!

Chapter 16

Maggie had volunteered to drive me home as I couldn't get hold of Mum to fetch me. As usual her phone was flat or lost. Our lane was littered with vehicles, and Maggie struggled to perform a twenty-three point turn between them. Unwilling to be parted from Dom again, Jen had left her car, promising to come for it soon. "Probably still in bed", Mum had remarked sourly and I chastised her for such crassness in front of a young and impressionable teenager (me). *Yeah, well, that was her reaction too!* Joe's Lurv Machine had been abandoned rather than parked on the grass verge which was gouged with tyre marks.

And yipeee! Gramps' sleek, clean, posh panther of a car was reclining neatly and precisely parallel with the hedge.

I didn't recognise a dirty red Volvo estate car. As I waved goodbye to Maggie, I peeped in through the back window and saw an array of spades and wellies and other gardening tools. Vaguely I remembered Mum mentioning having contacted a landscape gardener to come and give her ideas.

Oh No! It was all coming back to me! He was called Tony; sharp as a box of knives, Mum referred to him as Ant the Plant (Ant short for Antony... hehehe... get it... nudge, nudge...) I had stalked away in disgust!

Fashion guru my mother isn't. She could have looked gorgeous in her floaty, flimsy dress and pretty strappy sandals; her long hair hanging loose and wavy down her back. Sometimes, even I have to admit that she's well - er... beautiful.

But. This is where I go all teenage brat and groan with frustration: on her head she wore a red baseball cap. Back to front. Urrrr!

Cucumber sandwiches and Pims, then? NOT!

Gramps and Mum were eating crisps straight from the packet and drinking cold cider. My Grandfather may be stinking rich (according to Mum) and drive an environmental blitz of a car, but he's not snobby.

"Darling!" he rushed across and almost suffocated me in a huge bear-hug that lifted me off the floor. "I believe you've got a job?"

"Only Saturdays... or sometimes Sundays instead if Beth's going to a show" I told him. "It's great! and I'm getting PAID as well as having lessons..."

"You don't need to get a job, you know" he said, drawing me over to the retro arrangement of chairs "I told you I'll give you an allowance..."

"This won't be like work" I assured him "and I shall learn so much..."

"You've never actually mucked out, have you?" Mum asked sweetly, hiding a vicious smile.

"Well... no... but it can't be that difficult, can it...?"

"Difficult...? No..." her suppressed grin reminded me of the shark in Jaws, circling the man-cage in deep water.

"What are you saying?" I demanded crossly.

"Nothing, darling... just don't wear your best clothes..."

"Stop teasing her" Gramps ordered. "It can't be any worse than shifting a year's droppings from the paddock over there"

"True" Mum reached over and rubbed my arm.

Feeling spiteful I snapped "Why are you wearing that silly cap?"

"A Travelodge full of midges decided to sculpt my head into a replica of the Elephant Man" She lifted her chin to show me her neck all red and blotchy with bites.

"Is Gran... er... Lilian here?" I swivelled round to peer at the house. Nervously. I expected her falsetto voice to 'cooo-eee' or carol 'hello there darlings' as she tip tapped on high-heels round the corner.

"No... er..." Gramps cleared his throat "she's gone to visit That Woman in hospital. I'm picking her up later.

"That woman? You mean Dad's... er...?" how do you refer to the Usurper of the Family Home – a strumpet... a slapper? Oops, treading into dangerous territory here. Mum's face was tight and hard; I swear I saw flashes of sulphur in her eyes.

"Mmmmmmm" Gramps avoided our eyes. "high blood pressure or some such. I understand they're keeping her in hospital for a few days to do checks on her and make sure the... a-hum... er... baby's alright"

After a very awkward silence, Mum chirruped "Anybody want another drink... cup of tea, Gramps? Sara?" but was interrupted by a man... and what a man! swinging like Tarzan through the remnants of our shrubbery.

I'd forgotten. Ant the Plant.

Interesting.

Even more interesting, Mum blushed when he appeared!

Clip-board in one hand and a tape measure in the other, he sauntered across the dusty lawn towards us. Fit! Or wot! Slender...tall... narrow hips... long legs in dark brown cords... dark hair which almost curled, and was too long to be fashionable (but Mum loves long hair on men!). His smile made my toes curl; Mum flushed scarlet and tried to hide it by swiping her hand over her face as though flapping midges away. Of course he was terribly old; maybe even older than Mum; but sometimes, in a man, that can be attractive – especially when it creates laughter lines round the eyes.

I'd once asked Mum if she would ever marry again and she'd laughed "duh! don't you know all the suitable men are either married or gay?"

Hmmm! Then I must find out whether this hotty is married or gay before I cast him in the role of my new father. No good wasting time on a dud, even if he is easy on the eye.

Gramps made a leisurely departure. I thought he hadn't noticed my mother's blushes, but he winked at me and said "Walk me to my car, button?"

"Wouldn't you mind?" I demanded when we were out of earshot.

"Your mother..." he paused, and for a moment I suspected he was struggling to control his voice "is the daughter I always wanted. She married that useless son of mine; BAD move! Now I want her to be happy. She's young (is she?) beautiful, got loads of personality, talented, and has an amazing daughter..."

"So... that's a no, then. No, you wouldn't mind?"

"No... I wouldn't mind. Would you?"

I stopped suddenly, trying to imagine Mum and I sharing our lives with a new man. Weird! Seriously Weird!

"I don't know..." I said "but first, I need to find out if he's married already. Or gay"

"No he isn't..." Gramps said.

"How d'you know? You didn't ASK him, did you?" I was scandalised.

"No... no...NO!" he laughed, "I introduced them... I've known him for years." His eyes were twinkling "he was married to my niece, but they divorced years ago... I think he's probably ready to... er... well... and gay he is not!"

At the kitchen sink, Joe and Wayne were washing their gungey paint brushes. "Have you finished?" I asked "and has Mum paid you?"

Muttered yurrsss. I always have the feeling when confronting the foxy eyes of these crass yoofs, that my personality must be centred midway between my shoulders and my waist. They seem incapable of meeting my eyes; I struggle to see anything attractive in that little pointy Vee at the neck of a polo-shirt. But hey! what do I know?

When the Lurv-bus had over-revved and rattled its way into the distance, I saddled my lovely Teddy and waved goodbye to the couple poring over sheets of graph paper which would one day metamorphose into a landscaped garden.

At first, I thought about my new Saturday job... and about Teddy... and learning to look after him properly and ride well. Gradually, my thoughts turned to Mum. Would she or wouldn't she? Tony seemed like a really nice guy... but so had Dad... once.

Toxic Tart in hospital, huh? I imagined Dad sitting at her bedside, holding her hand, and laying his hand on her bump to feel the baby kicking. Just as he had probably once done when I was still an unborn blob.

For the first time, I could inwardly see him. Maybe I've been too angry to feel his reality. He's become a sort-of prop at which I can aim my rage.

But there he was again, my dad; real... a bit stiff, a bit formal... always (he thinks!) Right. I'm not sure I ever really liked him. But I LOVED him.

Lulled by the rhythmic clip clop of Teddy's hooves, I examined my mental picture of my father. In some ways, I missed him; yet... yet... I felt as though a fresh breeze had entered my being once he was gone. A lightness of being. I didn't have to try as hard. Or achieve as much.

I could actually have fun. There was no end to strive for; the doing and the being and the end product were all there to be enjoyed.

I don't have to be so serious about everything.

Poor baby. How will it cope with him? Maybe I shall have to become a step-sister to it after all – to help it to lighten up so that it won't be stifled.

Crazy spring!

What magical light has transfigured my life?

Only a few weeks ago I thought living in the country would be a black hole of boredom. Now, I hardly have time to breathe; the air is rarefied – no, the quality of life is rarefied. Everything sparkles with possibilities.

The golden light of sunset drifts around us as we move together, my pony and I, through mist and midges. Teddy tosses his mane. I lean forward and lay my cheek against his crest, stroking his silky neck. Ah, but touch is a wonderful thing!

Teddy pricks his ears, one swivels back to latch onto this strange noise I'm making. "It's laughter" I tell him. "Get used to it!"

More titles from **Forelock Books**:

'All that Glitters' by KM Peyton

'A Year at the Yard' by Ken Lake

'Finders Keepers' by Maggie Raynor

'One Good Turn' by Ruth Benton-Blackmore

'Pony Tails' by Sue Jameson

'Beside Me' by Carolyn Henderson

'Pony Racer' by Lucy Johnson

'Spirit and The Magic Horsebox' by Laura Quigley

'Spirit and The Shadow Stallion' by Laura Quigley

'The Horse with Big Hair' by Sally Burrell

'Legend... a true story' by Elizabeth Spencer

Visit *www.forelock-books.co.uk* for further information.